Whisper... He Might Hear You

Whisper... He Might Hear You

A Novel by

WILLIAM APPEL

DONALD I. FINE, INC.

New York

Appel, William.
Whisper—he might hear you : a novel / William Appel.
p.   cm.
ISBN 1-55611-190-8
I. Title.
PS3551.P556W44   1991   90-55081
813'.54—dc20   CIP
Manufactured in the United States of America

10 9 8 7 6 5 4 3 2 1

Designed by Irving Perkins Associates

ACKNOWLEDGMENTS

A special word of gratitude to my dear friend and colleague Sandra Berkley whose support and assistance and comradeship over the course of my entire career has made the difficult times more bearable and the high points even more joyful. *Merci,* Sandy.

For what he has helped me to discover about myself and life I want to thank Denis Walsh, the most healing person I've ever known.

For their continued help, thank you Ben Aliza, Marilyn Pessin, Karen and Marc Weiss, Norma Liuzza, Hy Steirman, Jack Kelly, and the members of my writing classes.

For her faith in this novel I want to thank my agent Jane Dystel.

For their superb editing, thank you Don Fine and Lizze Fitzgerald.

For her assistance with research about autism, thank you Dr. Anne Donnellan.

For his assistance with research, thank you Special Agent Roy Hazelwood of the F.B.I.'s Behavorial Science Unit at the F.B.I. Academy.

For his assistance with research, thank you Lieutenant Bob Ost of the New York State Troopers.

For Denise
Omygod!

. . . they were confronted with a murder of no ordinary character, committed not from jealousy, revenge or robbery, but with motives less adequate than many which still disgraced our civilization, marred our progress, and blotted the pages of our Christianity.

The Times (London), Sept. 27, 1988

Whisper... He Might Hear You

PART 1

CHAPTER ONE

THIS time he couldn't find one before he had swelled to bursting with his need of a death.

No, he thought, as he made one last adjustment to the blond wig on his shaved head. It was a matter of finding each other. She who must die and he who must kill her.

He ran his hands fastidiously over his body to see if he had shaved all the hair. Paid special attention to his pubic area.

He was prepared to spend all of himself searching for the next to die. But it was getting more difficult. It had taken six days this time.

A gust of November wind rattled an open window in the next room of the suite. He slipped on a silk robe and went to shut it. The wind had smelled coppery like the scent of blood, which reminded him of the last one—Marilyn? Maryanne?—and he felt keen, familiar anticipation in his groin.

The draft from the window chilled him. He poured twenty-year-old Scotch into a glass from a crystal decanter that stood on a silver filigreed tray. Sat staring out the window at a barge coming up the East River, remembering. Nothing could eradicate the childhood he had endured. But at least the huge inheritance from his parents gave him the freedom to pursue his missions.

All the walls were bare and stark white. The furniture, although expensive, was coldly modern. The suite gave no clue of ever having been lived in.

Madeline—that was it! He could see the pulse in her throat and remembered suddenly and completely the taste of salt and blood on her skin. He had wanted to be bathed in her wetness, to have her pressed into an unguent which he could rub on every part of his body, an elixir he could drink.

He drained his glass and set it down. As he punched out the newest one's number on the white touch-tone phone his lungs were aching.

"Hello?"

At the sound of her voice his chest constricted. It was just as he remembered: low pitched, throaty, with a tendency to raspiness. He placed the receiver back in its cradle.

She was home.

Lov-er-ly.

With her voice still resounding in his ears he took a stepstool from the pantry and carried it to the walk-in closet in his bedroom.

Pushing aside the suits and sport coats hanging on the rack he climbed the stool. When he could touch the ceiling he reached into his back pants pocket and took out a calendar card from a lizard-skin case. He measured off an outstretched palm and a half from the top of the ceiling and from the furthest point to the right. Then he held the card up against the designated spot.

There followed a clicking sound like some copy machines make when ejecting a sheet of paper. He started

4

counting as the ceiling opened in the center and its two halves began to recede. When he reached eight the ceiling had vanished.

He boosted himself up and sat on the lip of the opening, keeping his head bowed beneath the true ceiling above. He took a penlight from his shirt pocket and flicked it on.

He moved the beam of light first to an attaché case, then to a salesman's sample case and finally to an over-sized sports duffle sack made of parachute cloth. Next to the sack was stacked a collection of uniforms. He searched till he found a blue jumpsuit with the word OTIS on the back. The name Cal was stitched in script over the right hand shirt pocket. He had picked a name similar to Carl, his own, to be sure he reacted to someone calling him. He then chose a pair of construction worker shoes, white socks, peaked cap and a Timex. Stuffed them all into the sack.

As he moved the beam to the left, he shifted his buttocks and nearly bumped his head. He cursed the previous tenant for his poor planning. The Waldorf Towers man who had shown him the closet said, "It doesn't rank with the Pyramids for engineering expertise, but you'll have to admit that as a hiding place for valuables it's pure genius."

He had considered hiring a carpenter to expand the headroom or even build an entire hidden room. But that would involve a witness. That was why he had learned to do all the carpentry and electrical work himself.

He shone the light on a shelf containing what looked like a collection of unrelated paraphernalia. Chose carefully the tools he would use this time and placed them in the sack.

Taking some tissues he tucked them in too. In other compartments he set with religious reverence a cellular phone, a custom-made folding parabolic microphone equipped with a voice-activated recorder and a dip filter to erase background noise, a pair of Zeiss 50X binoculars, a Heckler and Koch P7 with a thirteen-shot clip and a custom silencer. As always, the lubricated condoms and the dental splint. Lastly, he packed his newly acquired weapon: an eight-inch survival knife.

He climbed down and shut the opening. Removed the blond wig and set it in the sack. Put on his everyday black wig, dressed and went to the elevator.

"Good evening, Mr. Nasson."

Carl Nasson nodded to the elevator man. Two women passengers, one middle-aged, the other in her mid-twenties, smiled at him. The younger woman couldn't keep from staring. Certainly his broad, rangy shoulders and surgeon's hands were attractive. But it was his face that held her attention. His delicately sculpted features were at odds with an exciting feeling she got from him. She continued to stare in an attempt to discover why she felt as she did.

Even his eyebrows seemed groomed. He was wearing a beige cashmere coat over a hard gray sharkskin suit. His shirt, which matched his eyes, was the palest shade of blue, and his tie appeared to have been cut from a bolt of jeweler's wine velvet. His navy kidskin shoes gleamed.

Despite his handsomeness, his perfect grooming and exquisite clothes, the young woman felt uneasy. His face looked honed. There seemed nothing extra or unnecessary about him. He had an air of extraordinary self-posses-sion—of not needing or wanting or caring about anything. She imagined his body, piercing as a knife.

The Art Deco lobby smelled of flowers, furniture polish, and a veritable explosion of perfumes and colognes. The gold leaf of the plaster ceilings shone in contrast to the darkness outside. Nasson looked at the four-faced Victorian clock: 6:01.

When his taxi arrived at the corner of Fifty-Ninth Street and Third Avenue he smiled, seeing that the falling snowflakes were unusually large. Heavy snowfalls kept people indoors, including police. More importantly, they muffled sound.

Nasson bought a ticket at Cinema One and went directly to the men's room. Inside a stall he unzipped the sack, took out a magnetic mirror and hung it on one wall. Stripped and pulled on the jumpsuit and work shoes. Replaced the black wig with the blond one and then set the peaked cap atop. Pasted on a blond walrus mustache.

Then he removed his blue contacts and inserted a hazel-colored pair. He stuck a plastic ink shield in his left shirt pocket containing four Bic ballpoints. Jammed two Phillies cigars in the other pocket. Removed his gold Rolex and replaced it with the Timex.

Looking into the mirror he grinned at the ingenuity of his disguise.

He found a phone outside. His heart ached when she didn't answer after four rings.

"Yes?" she finally said.

Relief flooded him. She was out of breath. Probably in the shower.

He pictured her good legs. Along his arms a sense of the weight of her legs, limp.

His hands were trembling as he hung up.

When he hailed a cab he delighted at the snow sugaring his shoulders. He didn't feel the cold. He was remembering the husky quality of her voice.

At the corner of Lexington and Sixty-Seventh he paid the cabbie and looked up at her white brick apartment house. Counted four stories down from the roof—her lights were on!

Lowering his gaze he went to the coffee shop across the street as planned.

"Two coffees to go, milk and sugar on the side, and two Danish."

The waitress stared at him invitingly. She was a pert blonde with an almost aristocratic fragility above the waist, thick peasant legs below. Her voice had a twangy sound which grated on his ears.

As he had rehearsed in his mind so many times, he went to the apartment building diagonally across the street.

The doorman, dressed like an admiral from an operetta, was studying the racing form hidden inside a copy of the *Post.*

Nasson stamped his feet on the carpet. "Fuckin' night, huh? Partner was supposed to meet me so I got an extra coffee and Danish. Whaddya say?"

"Yeah. Thanks, bud, but—"

"I'm with Otis. We got a report to check out the stress on the cables on number two bank. That was this afternoon. Need forty hours in a day to do it all. Especially in this snow. Wonder if they'll close the trots tonight."

"The day man didn't say nothing about no elevator trouble . . ."

Nasson almost couldn't wait to deliver the piece of research he knew would be the *coup de grace:*

"Harry must be getting old."

The doorman beamed and reached out for the bag containing the coffee and Danish. "Ain't that the truth."

On the twenty-sixth floor Nasson slipped on a pair of surgical gloves, opened a door marked STAIRCASE and settled himself in front of a window. For a big man he was agile.

From behind one of the walls came two sounds: the news on TV, and the muted thump of popular music. Slowly, savoring the act, he took the binoculars out of the sportsack and raised them in the direction of the building across the way.

The young woman was seated on the floor of the bedroom, legs spread wide, feet out. There were canvas weights attached to her legs. She was bending from the waist, touching right hand to bare left toes, arms windmilling high in the air.

A ballet.

She wore a leotard, cut high to the hipbones, tight between her legs. A soft mound there.

Beneath his shirt his chest bone gathered perspiration and he felt sweat run down the calves of his legs.

Her body was that of a young dancer, long-legged, hard, with flat rump, muscled thighs, slim arms, small conical breasts and a defined break between ribcage and waist.

Suddenly she ended her toe-touching, folded her legs, bent forward and rose to her feet without raising her hands for support. In one flowing motion she removed her clothing and stood gazing at her body in a full-length mirror. He was astonished by his good luck.

She lifted her shoulders, stomach tucked in, and twisted slightly to see the effect. Extending her chest, she cupped her breasts and pushed them higher and close together forming a valley.

The ache below his navel grew. His mouth felt metallic.

She looked over her shoulder and slapped her buttocks, waiting for ripples which didn't come. Then she squatted, knees spread, the pose ugly—and exciting.

He put a trembling hand on the wall, watching, staying in the shadows.

Here on the twenty-sixth floor she was so certain she was alone and unseen. As always one of the best parts was the spying, watching them unaware. It was at these times that they did the most exciting things—he'd once watched one masturbate with a vibrator dipped in cold cream. Later, he had picked her lock and . . .

9

But that was then.

Now she was out of his view, leaving him staring, shaking, mouth dry.

He grew empty above his abdomen, filled to splitting below.

Nasson took the phone out of the sack, his excitement barely controllable. Before he dialed he shoved tissue into both cheeks to make his voice hollow.

She answered the phone from the other room.

"Hello?"

Red hot silky fuck of a voice.

"Hello, Melanie."

"Who is this?"

"My name isn't important. I know all about you, Melanie."

"Who the hell is this?"

"I know that you're twenty-three, you weigh a hundred and eighteen, you wear a thirty-four B cup and you went to the University of Maryland. There's a mole on your left buttock and—"

His head jerked back from the sound of the phone slamming down.

When she didn't come back into view after a few moments, he pulled out the parabolic mike and pointed it in the direction of her apartment. After he had selected her voice from the many sounds coming from the apartments on her floor, he censored all but her's.

"L-look, officer, there's some nut calling me up who knows I have a mole on my tush and you tell me I have to come in and file a complaint!"

"Sorry, lady, regulations."

"Regu—never mind." She slammed the phone down.

"Operator, someone's giving me a hard time over the phone."

"Call the Customer Service Bureau, please. Three-nine-five-two-three-zero-zero."

Click.

She dialed.

"Yes. I want to report an obscene phone call."

"Your number please?

"Six-eight-four-zero-three-zero-one."

"Please call the Annoyance Call Bureau. Five-six-seven-nine-nine-three-zero."

Finally.

"Sorry, we're closed on weekends but we'll be open first thing in the mor—"

Click.

Nasson smiled as he dialed.

"Hello, Melanie."

"My God—what do you want?"

"I have what I want. I'm going to give you the honor of contributing your ultimate possession to me—your life. Don't waste your time and energy. There's nothing you can do, nowhere you can go where I won't—"

He could hear his heart as she hung up. Was she still naked as she spoke to him?

The sound of another woman's voice over the mike brought him back to the moment. "Slow down, Melanie, I can hardly understand you. How many times has he called?"

"Once he hung up. Twice I spoke to him. Oh, Nora, I'm so scared."

"When is your brother coming home?"

"Not till tomorrow."

"I'll send Frank over to bring you here for the night. Let the creep try and mess with the ex-heavyweight champ of the Sixth Fleet."

"Oh, thanks, Nor. How will I know Frank?"

"Right, you never did meet him. He'll wear a blue

11

parka, with ski tags from Vermont. Oh—his last name's O'Rourke. He should be there in ten minutes, okay?"

"Don't hang up, please, Nora. I'm very shaky."

"Look, you go have a drink and try to take some deep breaths. I've got to tell Frank what's up and give him the address. Call you back in one."

Nasson packed his gear and made his way to the elevator.

"All done already?" the doorman said.

"Don't take long when nothin's wrong. Thanks pal. 'Night now."

" 'Night."

Outside he was pleased to see that the snow was ankle deep. He crossed the street in long strides to work off tension and ease the ache in his groin.

A little while later Nasson spied a man through the glasses as he passed under a streetlamp coming from the west. About a half block away. His size gave him the appearance of an armoire on legs. Ski tags were attached to his parka.

Nasson began walking toward Frank O'Rourke.

As he drew within a few feet he became aware of just how huge O'Rourke was. He guessed about six-foot-four and at least two hundred and fifty pounds.

Nasson pretended to walk drunkenly. As he came abreast of O'Rourke he raised his head.

"Hey pal-ly," he shouted over the wind, "spare change for some soup?"

As O'Rourke reached a paw into his pants pocket he averted his eyes, chin tucked into his scarf.

Nasson looked all about—there was no one in sight—then threw the blow.

O'Rourke's head hit the concrete under the snow. Even over the wind Nasson had heard the snap of the light bone between the man's eyes. O'Rourke was dead before he hit

the sidewalk, the chop having crammed everything up-
wards into his brain.

Nasson dragged the body into an alleyway and behind
some garbage pails. Removed his blond wig and mustache
and contact lenses and placed them in the sportsack.
Stepped out of his jumpsuit and dressed himself in the
dead man's parka and scarf. Set and adjusted his black
wig.

By the time Nasson left the alleyway Frank O'Rourke
was already nearly buried under snow.

One block away from the new one's place he brushed
snow from cars till he found a four-door sedan. Reaching
into the sportsack he pulled out the gun, wrapped the
butt in a handkerchief and smashed the passenger window. Then he opened the door and tossed the sack inside.

He counted the number of cars from the corner. He
would need to distinguish the right one, even if it was
again covered with snow.

In moments Nasson stood before the doorman in the
new one's building. He kept his head down and the scarf
over his mouth as he spoke.

"Melanie Hines, please, Frank O'Rourke calling," he
said with a hint of an Irish lilt in his voice.

The doorman, who had a nose like a spigot, pressed one
of the many buttons on a console to the left of where he
sat.

"A Mr. Frank O'Rourke to see you, Miss Hines."

Nasson lifted his head just enough to see the doorman
look him over and say, "Yes, he is."

She had asked how he was dressed. Nasson had to contain a smile.

"Twenty-six E, Mr. O'Rourke."

In the elevator Nasson's legs were quivering and he
promised them that if they would be still a little while
longer the energy would soon be released.

When he rang her bell she answered immediately.

"Who is it?"

Hardly more than a whimper. The back of his neck got very warm.

He felt her eye through the peephole, then the sound of chains and bolts.

When she opened the door her green eyes were filled with fear. This fear and the narrow place above her upper lip, soft and delicate and vulnerable as a petal, seared him.

"Thanks for coming."

A voice like down feathers now. But he knew what evil hid behind their syrupy sounds.

"Come in please. God, I'm happy to see you, Frank. Would you like some coffee?"

"Thanks, we better be going," he said, lilting his tone. Her clean scalp glistening in the part of her hair and the tiny droplets of perspiration at her temples pierced him.

He watched her go to a white wrought iron coatrack and put on a camel toggle coat with a six-foot wool scarf crisscrossing her throat. He found himself breathing for her.

"I'm sorry for behaving like such a coward." She pulled on a wool cap and opened the door.

"Who wouldn't be scared in your place?"

She smiled at him as she locked the door.

In the elevator she stood so close to him he could feel her warmth.

"I really appreciate your coming out in this storm, Frank."

"Cold works up an appetite."

When they stepped off the elevator she turned to the doorman.

" 'Night, Miss Hines."

" 'Night," they said in unison.

Nasson's heart swelled from the thrill of getting past the doorman with her.

The winds made it almost impossible to keep their eyes open. They were the only two humans for as far as he could see.

He placed his arm in hers.

"Here, let me help you," he said taking a good grip. "After all, we wouldn't want anything to happen to you. Anything that might interfere with what I promised you over the phone."

"Oh my G—"

He slapped his hand over her mouth.

"One word, and you'll be swallowing your tongue. Understand?"

He took his hand away.

"I—y-yes, yes. I understand."

He grabbed her hand and dragged her to the four-door sedan. Brushed off some snow. The rust spots along the chrome looked like sores.

She tried to pull away and he squeezed her hand till the pain made her fall to her knees.

"B-broke my hand."

"You won't need it."

He reached through the broken glass and opened the car from within. Pushed her into the back.

"Please, God—help me, somebody!"

He brought his hand down across her face.

"God, please," she wailed.

"One more. One syllable above a whisper and you're done."

There was blood at the corner of her mouth. The snow had re-covered the car.

"Please," she whispered, "don't hurt me. I'll do anything."

Anything. He couldn't keep from smiling.

15

"Take off your clothes. Quick!"

In the cramped space she struggled out of her coat.

"Hurry," he commanded.

After she pulled off her sweater she gasped, seeing the surgical gloves under his wool ones. Nearly fainted when he took a clear plastic molding of teeth and palate and fit it into his mouth.

She maneuvered her slacks off. Removing her bra, she avoided his eyes.

He grasped one of her nipples.

She drew a deep breath. Held it. Exhaled. Another breath.

Holding her throat in one hand, he squeezed her nipple with slowly mounting pressure.

Her groan rose to a cry and she kicked frantically.

"Stop or I'll snap your neck!"

She grew limp.

He eased his grip.

She waited.

"Turn over."

She stared back, eyes glazed. Then slowly, she obeyed. Now the rest.

Hands trembling, he removed her panties. Slid down and felt her tuft as soft as rabbit's fur. Then he placed his cheek against her right buttock, reached up and clasped a hand over her mouth.

He bit with slowly increasing pressure. If only he could feel her flesh without the constraints of the splint. But then his saliva could be DNA-tested.

When he stopped and removed his hand, she was crying.

He unzipped his pants. Unwrapped a condom, slipped it on.

His pulse battered at his temples. Reached into the

16

sportsack till he felt the handle of the knife. Hate and lust turned his eyes red. The taste of blood rose on his tongue.

He raised the blade and brought it down with all his might.

CHAPTER TWO

D R. Kate Berman handed Chief of Detectives Bill Casey a glass of water in which two Alka Seltzer tablets were fizzing. The Chief downed the drink with an expression so grim that she had to smile, though she had steeled herself against his visit. She knew why he had come.

Although his presence triggered a set of old fears, she was delighted to see him. Twenty-three hundred detectives under his command. Third in the history of the Department for total number of citations earned. Yet here he sat with his incorrigible cowlick springing up, an expression on his sixty-one-year-old face that said he was in need of a warm bottle of milk, a change of diaper or a nap. Cranky as ever. She studied him. His hair was the color of water in a canteen. Skin was creased as an old wallet. Gnarled features. His washed-out blue eyes sagged at the far corners as if pulled down from innocence into cynicism. Bruised . . .

Casey looked around the pleasant room filled with comfortable furniture, firelight, cluttered bookshelves and cut flowers. He felt he was back in the Berman brownstone in Manhattan instead of their house in upstate Rhinebeck.

"They've all been killed in the city so far," he said.

"I don't want to be filled in on things like this anymore, Bill. I know something about it, of course. Can't read a paper or watch the news—"

"This makes number eight."

He waited.

"You don't need me. You have a task force the size of an army. You have the FBI's new national data computer on violent crime, Stern at Harvard, Walsh at Pennsylvania."

"I need you all right."

"What about this new DNA profiling where they can I.D. someone from his semen, blood, saliva or a single hair?"

"What about it is, this guy must wear gloves, leaves no blood or hairs, uses a condom—lubricated yet. And—get this—forensics says he uses some kind of doohickey in his mouth so there's no saliva." He shot up from his chair. "The best damn criminologist in the whole country, and she's writing books about autistic kids."

"I'm very happy, thank you, Bill."

"Sorry, didn't mean to raise my voice. You got hurt last time. You're scared. I know. I understand. But you're fine now."

"I want to stay that way."

"You think I like coming here begging? You're the best. You don't think like other people. I don't even know how you come up with your psychological profiles. I don't want to know."

"That's because you don't approve, you old flatfoot."

"Wrong. I approve of anything that would get this guy."

"How do you know it's a guy?"

"Are you saying you think it's a woman?"

"I'm not saying anything, Bill."

"Neither is this freak. Know what we know after eight victims?"

"I'm not in the mood for mysteries."

"I'll tell you."

"I can't wait."

"He's a biter."

Like the last one, she thought. And her mind hurtled back to that most terrible of times when she had seen the killer's blade enter her and, after, the strange flowerlike stain like a melted red anemone spread on the waist of her dress. Bleeding like a sprung leak. Blood like warm syrup oozing from her hands. Smelling the smell of herself and feeling her eyes focusing on a blade of grass, a tiny insect, and thinking how that would be the very last thing she'd ever see, *that* blade of grass, *that* insect.

"Kate?"

"Sorry."

"I'll tell you what else we know after eight murders."

"Please don't."

"Zip. Women from age twenty-two to sixty-four. Each had different looks, different things they did for a living. No eight women ever had less in common. Six different kinds of weapons. Even different methods. Once he's ritualistic, next he's a butcher, then you'd think he was a surgeon. Only way we know it's the same guy is the matching bite marks. Not only can't we I.D. him from dentition 'cause we have no sheet on him, but forensics says he could easily have changed his dentition with that thingamajig he uses in his mouth. Besides, there's no getting into this guy's head."

"You can always get into their heads."

She saw a light go on behind his eyes. Hopefulness and humility were appealing in such an old warhorse and friend. His need tugged at her.

"Just a peek at the evidence . . . ?" he urged. "Please, I'm drowning, Kate."

She held out for a few seconds more.

"Just one," she finally said, full of dread.

CHAPTER THREE

"'**M**ORNING ma'am," said the detective who was Casey's driver as he opened the rear car door.

Kate strode out of her carriage house. Her gait, were it not for her woolen cap, would have made her hair bounce. It was the walk of a woman who exuded confidence. Except for the tiny wrinkles at the corners of her eyes, she looked more like a graduate student than a forty-three-year-old woman. Yet, as Casey studied her from his window, he saw that there was a hesitancy in her stride which hadn't been there before she was attacked by the "Central Park Ripper."

"Coffee?" Casey asked extending a Styrofoam container. "I got yours. Black, still?"

"Right," she said sliding in.

As the car pulled away Casey told her all he knew and theorized about the latest murder. Kate made mental notes.

"So," she said, "no bug in the woman's apartment. The killer used a wireless phone to call her and then a parabolic mike to hear her speaking to her girlfriend?"

"Only way he could've known the girlfriend was sending her boyfriend over to protect her. And you should see the size of this guy O'Rourke."

"You've got some smart, strong, evil bastard on your hands, Bill."

"Tell me about it."

Kate wasn't interested in talking to either of the doormen in the two buildings. Nor to the victim's girlfriend or the waitress who had waited on the killer. Casey could handle all that.

Instead, she began her walk-through, trying to hear what Casey referred to as her "inner voices."

As she entered the elevator of the apartment building across the street from the murdered woman's, she was filled with a familiar thrill and dread.

Kate never knew how much exhilaration came from the possibility of finding new evidence, how much from the vicarious thrill of pretending to be a murderer. Or of trying to imagine the primal pain driving the killer, the surge of power he felt as he played out the drama of his crime.

The feeling always frightened her. It was like entering an area of madness in herself. There was an awful excitement to it, too, something she both loathed and enjoyed.

She remembered telling her husband about the first time she had walked through a crime scene:

"I was struck by how intoxicating it must have been for him."

"A real spine tingler," he had teased. "Looked into necrophilia? How about cannibalism?"

"Really, Josh, I feel that if I can get into the madness, the thrill, the madman'll be revealed to me. Killings for money or anger are easy—the motives I mean. But this.

23

There's passion here. Passion and rage and . . . precision."

"I'd come down off this, Kate. Trying to feel what the
killer felt. Hating, so you can identify with him. Kind of
stuff can make you crazy."

Now as Kate stepped off the elevator she felt a stab of
fear. Remembering where Casey believed the killer had
stood when he made his phone call to his victim, she
forced herself to go there.

Arriving at the stairwell she took out a pair of binoculars from her bag, raised them to her eyes. Looked at the
murdered woman's window, trying to psych herself up.

I'll get her soon, she made herself think.

Nothing.

She needed to feel his compelling desire and hatred for
the dead woman. Not knowing what commonality linked
the victims made it especially hard to conjure the killer's
feelings.

In the soundless stairwell her ears began to ring. Infuri-
ating when she was trying to concentrate.

She put the binoculars down. Trying to will his hatred
and desire made her feel as though she had stepped into
an elevator with no flooring. At the same time she was
filled with pity for the dead woman.

Kate took the elevator down.

*I'm going to kill this Frank O'Rourke who's coming to
protect her from me so I can do what I came here to do.
How confident I feel.*

She was beginning to get inside him.

But she still felt more victim than killer.

Outside, Kate wished it would snow. She took out the
map Casey had given her. Went to the alleyway where
the shape of the body was outlined in chalk. The murderer would have to be very powerful to kill such a big
man with his bare hands.

24

She made herself stand in the alleyway till she had summoned his pride and excitement at the power and skill needed to kill such a large man. In doing so, she scared herself. Her ability to get into the murderer's mind so quickly now alarmed her.

It's only the dark side of myself. Everyone has a place where they meet their own demons.

She would run through this scene and the others. Tell Casey her feeling and try to go back to writing her book.

She was eager to finish the run-through. It was becoming easier to imagine what the killer felt. A feeling of unexpected good luck spread through her. She imagined exchanging the jumpsuit for O'Rourke's ski parka.

Her legs trembling with excitement, she hurried to the apartment of the dead woman.

Kate stared at the sealed apartment, feeling him try to decide whether to kill right there. He must have enjoyed the look of relief on Melanie's face that decided it for him. Melanie would be even more relieved when he took her outside.

And what a feeling of power and invincibility he must have had, walking past the doorman with her! But were those enough reasons for risking taking her out into the snowstorm when he could kill her in the warm apartment?

Leaving the building, Kate stood outside, feeling him welcome the snowstorm which would deafen sound, impair vision and empty the streets of witnesses.

Now she relished the look of terror on Melanie's face as she learned who was really inside the ski parka.

Anticipation was making it hard for Kate to breathe. She looked at Casey's map. Made her way over to the actual scene of the crime.

There was so much blood on the rear seat of the sealed car that the crime-scene people had had to use tape instead of chalk. How astonishing it always was to see how much blood the human body contained!

Kate bit her lower lip. Closed her eyes and smelled the blood. She could hear begging in the air. There was a rush of triumph. *How perfect!* She didn't know if this last thought was hers or the killer's.

Panic filled her. She had to lean against the car. She pushed a fist into the pit of her stomach to unlock her diaphragm.

In a few moments the natural rhythm of her breathing returned. It was then she realized it had really begun snowing.

Good. It will absorb her screams, she thought, and retched on the curb.

CHAPTER FOUR

KATE watched Humphrey Bogart and Claude Rains walk off into the distance. The music rose, then the TV screen went blank.

Her husband Josh had switched it off. He said, "I never would've let Ingrid go. Shoot her husband—Claude Rains too—and on the plane with my girl."

Kate had been disturbed for the last twenty-four hours since walking through the crime scene. But Josh's romanticism and humor lightened her darkness.

She laughed with him. How she loved to watch him laugh. He wore an expression of such genuine joy, such surrender.

"You're something, you are," she said.

She studied him as he rose and ejected the tape from the video recorder. He was a mountain of a man. His weathered, earnest features had the reflective look of a person who had both suffered and enjoyed a great deal, who was prepared for the worst and hoped for the best. At forty-nine he still had a posture which helped conceal the twelve pounds of new fat that had won out over old muscle.

Josh said, "Anyway . . ."

"Anyway, what?"

"Anyway, nothing. It's a conversation starter."

"Glib."

"I've been rehearsing all day."

She had noticed how many married women went about creating their husbands. My husband, they'd say, can't stand small talk. He likes me to wear beige all the time. He would murder me if I had one puff of a cigarette. He won't eat frozen foods. This way bewildered lovers and friends were made into husbands. She wanted a man who didn't have to be changed. Who was already complete and confident and in some ways would always be mysterious to her.

She said, "Did I tell you I adore you?"

"Not today."

"Consider it said."

His wife's hand was in his. Her once precise features were softening with time. She was still beautiful, but what Josh saw in her was beyond beauty. He was moved by her vulnerability, the air of a girl that belied her age. He remembered first seeing her intelligent, thoughtful eyes and discovering something he had always wanted. She seemed more fully alive and wide awake than most people. The new darkness around her eyes, which he knew came from the crime-scene walk-through, twisted his heart. He turned his face to prevent her seeing his expression.

"What?" she said.

Too late, he thought. She was so sharp.

"Nothing," he said.

"Okay, don't tell me. You think Susan's lasagna was as good as mine?"

"No," he lied. "Excellent, but not as good. You lost a few pounds."

"Does it show—wait a minute. Tell me what your sad expression was about earlier."

"I told you."

"You told me nothing."

Kate watched him rise and go to a built-in liquor cabinet under the floor-to-ceiling bookshelves and pour two snifters of brandy. He had a way of making ordinary objects seem tiny, like the way his huge hands now cradled the snifters as if they were pony glasses.

She thought about how sensitive he was under his enormous frame and rumpled clothing. How he could cry without embarrassment.

When he handed her a snifter she said, "I shouldn't let you off the hook so easily. But whenever I find a decent, straight lay with a great tush, I do what I can to make it work."

He smiled, bent down and kissed her.

"Want to do something good for your cardiovascular system?" she said.

"Is this a trick question?"

They broke into laughter. Almost at the same instant the phone intercom buzzed. Kate picked up the receiver. It was their Saturday cleaning woman.

"If I'm not interrupting, we're done down here."

"We" meant Addie and her fifteen-year-old daughter, Toby.

"We'll come down and get out of your way," Kate said.

As Kate and Josh reached the bottom of the stairs they met Toby carrying a vacuum cleaner.

"Hi!" the girl said.

Physically the girl was a teenage version of her mother: petite, dark, endlessly energetic. But while Addie was a hard shell with sweet nutmeats, Toby was sweet through and through.

29

Josh cupped Toby's face in his huge hand. Kate slipped her a pair of earrings she had seen the girl admiring.

"I can't."

"I already asked Mom if it was okay," Kate said.

She was surprised by the strength of the slight girl's hug. Toby scampered upstairs to a mirror.

Addie appeared so quickly she seemed to be playing an older Toby in a play with little or no transition.

"Emmet was supposed to take her to the mall yesterday. Did he remember? *Shoot*—he hardly remembers me from the wedding."

Josh pinched Kate, prolonging their laughter. They both adored the cleaning woman, who tried to conceal her generous nature behind a crusty mask.

Addie said, "Now don't trash this place, you two. I'm getting too old for this big house."

Looking about the living room, Josh marveled at how spotless the place looked. He had thought it perfectly clean before. He could not believe he was lucky enough to have a cleaning woman who could even build a fire.

Kate smiled because under Addie's hand everything had acquired the sheen of loving care. Kate loved this room. Its enormously high ceilings made it rather austere, but it was saved from somberness by the cheerful furnishings. Bookshelves covered much of the walls and framed the doorway.

The furniture was a hodgepodge of old and heirloom and new which had been more collected than selected. Chippendale butted with Oriental, country French with Victorian. A congenial, lived-in room. The earth tones of drapes and upholstery were inviting. The ancient Persian rug was subdued with wear. Lamps as well as firelight threw a yellow haze on brass, on watercolors and on oversized glass ashtrays. The chairs and couches were large and comfortable. Nothing looked intended for show. Comfort and mellowness created its own style.

Kate took her favorite seat in a floral patterned chair. Josh relaxed in a wing chair and ottoman covered in ox-blood leather with brass studs.

Neither saw the stranger who hid outside their window.

CHAPTER FIVE

"I want to go to college, Kate. I want to be a psychologist like you," the teenager said in a loud, unmodulated voice. They sat opposite each other in Kate's office in the Summerfield Institute in Rhinebeck.

Kate smiled. Very few students with autism managed to enter high school. Even fewer got to college. Those who did usually majored in math or computer studies, not psychology. There was no reason, though, for Lilah not to be given a chance. Lilah was one of those rare people who, in great part, manage to overcome autism. She was also a savant—she remembered how many inches she'd left the door to her room ajar and if even one paper clip had been moved or removed.

"I still don't know what it means when people are silent in conversation," Lilah said with little inflection and no rhythm. "They tell each other things with their eyes and I don't know what they're saying or thinking."

Kate saw the girl was upset. She said, "I was thinking of how far you've come, how proud of you I am."

"Will you give me your recommendation?"

"Absolutely. You can start helping your chances, though, by concentrating on lowering your voice."

"I know . . . I forget. Anything you say."

How special this darling girl was. She accepted her oddities and peculiarities of speech and manner. She regarded them simply as problems to be overcome, though others would be self-conscious or embarrassed.

Kate wanted to hug her. She knew the girl ached to be hugged—loved. She also knew, though, that Lilah sometimes suffered from painful oversensitivity, even when her mother, the singer Joni Freemont, touched her.

Later in the day Kate made some notes she hoped to use in the book she was writing about autism.

   . . . Perhaps the most difficult obstacle for children like Lilah is the cruel kindness well-intentioned people employ to protect them from expectations that might be destroyed by their autism. Lilah has shown unequivocally that there is hope for children suffering from this disorder —that genuine, consistent caring, acceptance, good teaching and appropriately high expectations and encouragement can help them to grow to their potential.

   I have watched Lilah struggle with her autism, sometimes in great confusion, often in much pain. In seeing her come to terms with it I know I've seen the human spirit at its best.

   As a criminologist I learned that to best understand the criminal we must recognize what is criminal and sociopathic, even psychopathic, in ourselves. In order to help children with autism participate in our social world, we must first see them in ourselves.

   For instance, I am very weak in mechanical and athletic skills, and I can't carry a tune. My math is so poor I barely got by, even with tutors and twice the effort of average students.

   After all, what is autism but a developmental disorder

33

with a primary problem in social interaction? And who of us is not lacking in some area of development and social interaction?

   Mozart, certainly a great genius, was not only undeveloped in many ways, his narcissism lost him his . . .

Just as she wrote those words, the first of a series of phone calls came which would forever change her life.

"Aunt Kate, you're on the front page of last week's *National Exposé!*"

It was her nineteen-year-old niece, Jenny.

"Really?" Kate said, not wanting to stifle the girl's excitement. She had been on the front of the news rag once before when she'd helped solve a multiple murder case. She had insulated herself against the brazen lies.

"Ginny saw it," the girl went on. "You know, I brought her home one weekend."

"Sure, honey, I remember."

"There's a picture of you talking to Chief Casey in the living room. Addie and Toby are in it too. Says you're going to be working with him to help catch that new serial murderer. And that Uncle Josh is the ex-medical examiner from the city and he's going to help, too. Is it true?"

"I don't think so. But I did walk through one of the crime scenes."

"Gross. You want me to mail you this copy?"

"Sure. Miss you."

"Me, too."

"When are we going to see our favorite person in the world?"

"Should be able to come home for a weekend soon. Whoever said sophomore year's easier than freshman didn't have my teachers."

Kate always felt pleasure when Jenny called their house

home. Since her brother-in-law's fatal heart attack seventeen years ago, following her sister's death the year before, she and Josh had raised the girl. She could not imagine either of them loving her more.

"Got to go, Aunt Kate, late for a class. Love you."

"Love you, sweetheart."

Kate placed the receiver back in its cradle, strode out of her office, out of the building and drove to the nearest newsstand.

When she read about how she had been quoted out of context, using her statements about a serial murder years ago, her anger made her bite down so hard the roots of her teeth ached.

Then she imagined the killer reading this story, and the old familiar fear pressed her lungs flat.

CHAPTER SIX

20 West Twentieth Street in Manhattan held a trendy, hi-tech Cajun restaurant. Also a methadone center. Neither was surprising on this long street between Fifth and Sixth Avenues. The surprise was the Westside Rifle and Pistol Range in the basement.

Nasson, wearing an army fatigue jacket, combat boots, yellow-tinted aviator glasses and mustache, swung the door open, walked past the elevators and down the stairs. He followed the corridor till he reached the range. There was the smell of gunpowder and a constant chorus of muted gunfire, duller than a firecracker, more resonant than an exploding tire.

People cleaned their weapons at a half dozen metal tables dispersed throughout the place. On the walls were reminders that all loaded firearms had to be pointed downrange at all times. Ads from Smith and Wesson, Beretta and Uzi. Framed charter club memberships from the National Rifle Association. Newspaper stories about armed citizens defending themselves successfully against muggers and burglars.

One of the instructors, Frank Nacarino, stood behind the cash register. A dustbroom-mustached Brooklyn Italian whose pudgy face was the color of wet sand on an overcast day, he was selling ammo to a man Nasson recognized as an off-duty detective.

Nacarino had told him that ten percent of the range's customers were police. Fed up with the long trip to the department's only range in the Bronx and its long lines, they preferred this place. How sweet it was for him to know he was so close to some of the men who undoubtedly were searching for him!

As Nasson waited he leaned against the showcase containing items for sale: holsters, oil cans, magazine speed loaders, eye protectors, ear plugs.

Nacarino handed Nasson ammo, a target, noise barriers that looked like headphones and his .38 Smith and Wesson model number 36. The gun was a snub-nose type police use off duty. It also delighted Nasson to be using a police gun.

Inside the shooting area he could feel the vibrations up through the soles of his boots. He set up his target, then used the crank to set it out at fifteen feet. He stood in the Weaver stance—aiming the gun with his right hand, left supporting right hand, body at a forty-five degree angle to the target. He focused on the front sight so it was perfectly in place, equally spaced from the sides and level across the top. He squeezed and the gun rose with the recoil.

When he'd finished an hour later, he cranked the target back in and took a seat by himself to clean the weapon.

As he returned the target and gun to Nacarino the instructor said, "*Madonna!* Ninety-three out of a hundred in the ten ring. You should be the one doing the teaching."

*   *   *

Nasson had just left the range and was waiting for a taxi in front of a newsstand. He glanced down at a stack of newspapers and froze.

There on the front page of *National Exposé* was the headline: CRIMINOLOGIST SAYS LADY KILLER HAS MIND OF TEN-YEAR-OLD.

He threw down a bill for the paper. Walked away turning to page two, not hearing the newsdealer calling after him about his change.

He studied the photographs of the criminologist, her medical examiner husband, the chief of detectives and the criminologist's housekeeper and the housekeeper's daughter.

He collided with a passerby wearing a Con Ed hardhat.

"Hey—you blind?" the beefy man shouted into Nasson's face.

Nasson shot his hand out to the man's face pressing two fingers against his eyes. "No, but you *will* be if you don't get out of my way *now.*"

The beefy man looked in the handsome face seeing a fury so out of proportion to the incident that the only explanation was madness.

"S-sure bud, sorry . . ."

Nasson went to a bar, ordered a Rob Roy and continued reading.

Dr. Berman says, "To better understand the serial murderer it is useful to compare him to some ten-year-olds: selfish, convincing liars, callous.

Ten-year-old!
He bolted the cocktail. Ordered another.

If he can be sure that negative consequences won't follow, he'll lie. Because he doesn't orient himself to the other person's point of view his interpersonal relationships are essentially constructed on benefits to himself. Because he is stunted in his maturity these benefits have to be fairly immediate. Brilliant ten-year-olds often score high on IQ tests, and are likely to appear more intelligent than normal thirty-year-olds, even though ten-year-olds can't think abstractly and many thirty-year-olds can. If we continue to make analogies between these two, we'll see that though the psychopathic killer is very intelligent he's also very naive.

Naive!

"A naive ten-year-old!" he said aloud to himself.

"Did you want another, sir?"

Nasson looked up seeing the waiter. "No. Just the check."

Again he studied the photograph of the criminologist. The arrogant cunt. He'd prove to her who the naive one was.

He reflected on the photograph of the cunt's housekeeper and her daughter. Then he tore out the pages containing the story and put them in his pocket.

He would walk home to calm himself. Too much adrenaline made one react instead of act.

He began to construct a plan.

Lov-er-ly.

CHAPTER SEVEN

KATE slammed the front door, which made Josh look up quizzically from his newspaper.

"What?" he said.

She tossed the copy of *National Exposé* into his lap.

Josh's eyes raced down the front page: YOKO SPEAKS WITH JOHN'S GHOST, FOOTBALL PLAYER GIVES BIRTH.

His eyes widened when he read, CRIMINOLOGIST SAYS LADY KILLER HAS MIND OF TEN-YEAR-OLD.

He studied the photographs of Kate, himself, Casey, as well as those of Addie and Toby.

Then he read the story.

"Who's the son of a bitch who quoted this old stuff?"

"That doesn't matter now. What if he sees this on a newsstand or on some convenience store rack? It's going to infuriate him. He's not going to know this toilet paper misquoted me and quoted me out of context, using things I said years ago about sociopaths, not psychopaths."

"Let's get out of here for a while. Someplace warm where we can hear the ocean from our window. That inn in Bermuda."

As if he hadn't spoken, Kate said, "You don't understand how his kind of mind works. We're all in danger. Even Addie and Toby. Got to warn them. What time is it?" She looked at her watch. "Toby's probably still in school. Have Addie's schedule somewhere in my desk. They've got to get out of Rhinebeck for a while. Addie has a sister in Florida and—"

"Take it easy now. I'll call Addie. And if it makes you feel better I'll pick Toby up from school. Here, sit down. I've got Addie's schedule in my address book."

She had just settled into her chair when the phone rang, lifting her inches out of her seat.

Josh picked up the receiver.

"Yes, this is he. *What?*"

His stricken tone made her tune in. She could feel the blood pumping in her neck, her stomach, her temple.

Then the words "Rhinebeck High School" hollowed her. Toby. He'd gone after Toby.

When Josh said in a cracked voice that he'd be right over, she knew for certain. No, she'd known from the first change in his tone.

When she finally could bear to look into his eyes, the bitter lump in her throat swelled to fill her chest, pushing her ribs against each other, crushing her heart to a kernel.

She went into his arms then, unable to cry. Not feeling solace in Josh's embrace was a new feeling and told her how devastated she was.

After a long while she said in a tone so mechanical it frightened Josh: "I'll tell Addie . . . if she doesn't already know."

CHAPTER EIGHT

J OSH sensed a vacantness, a loss. Opened his eyes and saw it was night and Kate was gone from their bed. What hell a bed is, he thought, when you can't sleep in it.

Normally he would be concerned if Kate, who usually slept soundly the moment her head was on a pillow, woke in the middle of the night. Not tonight.

"Go back to sleep, hon," he heard her say quietly.

He turned and saw her curled up in a window seat holding a snifter of brandy.

"Can I get you anything?" he said.

"Brandy's good. Knits my soul."

She was slurring her words.

"Going to help Casey find the bastard who did this," she said.

"Lost your mind?" he blurted and immediately regretted it.

"Why—you find one, Josher?"

He knew now that she was more high than he had realized. And he was filled with tenderness that she had called him by his pet name.

He turned the nightstand lamp on low and studied her. Her face showed the strains of the last few days: the phone call to Addie, the funeral, the newspaper headlines and TV special editions. He had never seen her look so vulnerable since . . . since that last maniac nearly killed her. Nor so old and young at the same time. The sight of her agreeably crooked little girl's feet drained his heart.

He climbed out of bed, lumbered across the room and sat behind her in the window seat, making a bow of himself against her back.

"You do whatever you have to do, Katie. Whatever you need from me, you got."

He knew from the subtle caving in between her shoulders that sobs were again rising in her throat.

She sank into herself, and he missed her.

They sat in the window till light hurt their eyes. Then they made their way through their morning, vaguely able to recall how it felt to be whole.

CHAPTER NINE

S ALES of door locks, burglar alarm systems, guard dogs and hand guns soared upstate as well as in New York City. Under Chief Casey's direction his special task force accelerated the arrests of known sex offenders, peepers, obscene phone callers and the like.

One TV station offered an 800 number to anyone having any information about what one *Post* reporter dubbed the "I Love New York Killer." The *Daily News* offered a ten-thousand-dollar reward. Ted Koppel did a show about whether the FBI should automatically be allowed to track a serial murderer who had restricted his crimes to one state.

That night Nasson watched Casey, the mayor at his side, wrap up a TV news conference.

Woman reporter: "Do you advise women to carry a billy club or Mace?"

Casey: "They're both illegal. But hair spray is good. You get that in your eyes it stings."

Woman reporter: "What about handguns?"

Casey: "We're trained. The public's not. You're dealing with a person who's very strong and cunning. Who's capable of taking a weapon away from you. We want you to keep from coming in contact with him. Or we want to see you get away. There's some prevention tips we've come up with which you can see on the display board behind us now. I'll read them aloud.

"One: Don't walk alone. Team up because there is strength in numbers. Two: Don't carry your keys in your purse. If they're stolen or lost, any I.D. will tell the attacker where you live, and the keys will provide easy access to your home. Don't place keys under mats or in mail boxes. Three: When you reach your home, have your keys ready. If you have to fiddle around you are giving someone a chance to sneak up on you. Four: Ask anyone claiming to be a police officer for a badge and an I.D. card. Five: Don't give out any personal information over the phone. Six: Never enter an elevator with a stranger. Seven: Make sure all locks work, and check to make sure windows and doors and garage doors are locked. Eight: When you go out, tell your neighbors where you are going and when you plan to return. Stick to these plans."

Casey turned and looked directly at the audience. "The main thing is common sense."

Nasson laughed out loud. Common sense against his genius! He pressed the remote off button and took a long swallow of his Rob Roy.

His need had intensified since killing the daughter of the cleaning woman of that pig. The girl hadn't possessed one molecule of the essences he required to ignite his desire and to demand its release. She had been only a canvas to spatter his fury at Kate Berman on.

Besides her filthy words, he despised the criminologist. He sensed she was hard-edged and purposeful. The investigation of bloodied and broken bodies was a province he considered exclusively for men.

Since the girl's death his untended need had been

45

mounting. Now it was nearly constant. Still, he hadn't been able to find a new one.

He saw an image of himself as a coiled beast waiting unseen on a much traveled path.

Outside Bloomingdale's the rain fell like a curtain of fine silver, walling Nasson deeper into the private chamber under his umbrella. He leaned his weight on his crutch, swung and pushed off toward the main entrance.

Even in Manhattan, he thought, smiling, people were compassionate to a person with a crutch and a foot in a cast.

Inside, he stopped and studied the mass of countless females in many sizes and shapes until they seemed to meld into the essence of the next one.

As he pretended to be shopping for a woman's watch, he became aware of the eyes of a tall filament of a woman resting on him. He guessed she was in her late twenties, pretty except for a slightly coarse complexion. Under her opened coat she was wearing beige widewale corduroy slacks with a tailored blouse of raspberry silk.

He saw the slim woman point to a particular tray of watches. Then her high-pitched voice assaulted his ears.

Behind a cosmetics counter stood an attractive young woman with a breezy smile and slightly teasing look who seemed to be especially full of life. He felt his heart had stopped.

"Can I help you?" she said in an irritating nasal drone, and he moved on.

He hobbled over to a perfume bar where a woman dressed in stone-washed jeans and a work shirt was dabbing the back of her wrists. Although she was obviously approaching middle age she had an unexpectedly young vitality.

She turned as he approached and he saw interest in her eyes. The clerk behind the counter asked if she needed any help.

"No thanks," he heard the woman answer in a hoarse, rich voice. A smoker's voice—once so common, now so unusual. She smiled at him.

His heart rose in his chest.

The clerk moved on to another customer. The youthful older woman, whom he now saw was slim but large-boned, turned to him.

"Here, I'll move aside so you can get closer to the counter."

Nasson gave her a smile so nice that it struck her as dazzling. He had a classic sort of handsomeness. She preferred a man who wore his good looks carelessly, like a favorite old pair of shoes. But this one was too gorgeous to ignore.

He stared at her, still not speaking.

"The strong, silent type, huh?"

"I'm sorry, I own a pet shop, and I spend a lot of time talking to terriers and guppies. Sometimes I forget how to talk to people."

He created another smile, more sincere than the last.

"Who's it for?" she said in her tantalizing voice.

For an instant he had an urge to crush her throat. He took a deep breath.

"Sorry?" he said.

"The perfume."

"Oh." He seized a chance to smile sheepishly. "It's my older sister's birthday." He had an idea this particular one would like that he bought expensive perfume for an older sister.

"Well, there's my favorite—*Bal à Versailles* . . ."

Her tone told him she was his. I am your future, he thought, and felt his pulse would explode.

Later, as she helped him into her car so that she could drop him off at his apartment before she went on to Lawrence, Long Island, she said huskily, "What's your name?"

"Cal," he said, thinking, I am A. Nonymous. And for one sublime day you have come into contact with genius.

Still later, when he suggested that they might have a drink outside the city, she noticed for the first time a unique hardness at the corners of his mouth that chilled her. A terrible intuition began to take shape.

"Where are we going?" she said in that deep voice that was at once so magnetizing and so repellent.

"All the way."

A trickle of sweat sprouted in her armpit. "I really think it might be better if we did this when I have more time." She shifted into third gear.

His face formed a smile so quick it seemed no more than a tic. She felt caught in an inexplicable down current, that she was sinking, pulled down by a great invisible power.

"I said I really think it might be better if—"

"I heard you. When I kill someone it's when *I* choose to."

His words, the matter-of-factness of his tone, pounded the air from her.

"Don't try anything," he said. "I have a gun aimed where you breathe."

She felt fastened to her seat, knowing suddenly who he was and unable to say or do anything. Time seemed to hesitate with her.

"P-please let me stop. I-I'm going to be sick."

"You're going to be more than that. Crack your window for some air."

She pressed one of the buttons on her door. "W-where are we going?"

The exact words he had asked so many years ago of Her

as she pulled him by his trembling little hand into Her bedroom. The intoxicating scent of Her perfume stung his nostrils. The fear and excitement and guilt he had felt then assaulted him. Hate splintered his eyes now. He blinked to see the road.

"A-are you all right?" Her sphincter muscle threatened to let go.

Are you all right, Carl baby? Here, don't be a scared puppy. You know how I make you feel good. You're not going to be sick again, are you doll baby?

He felt the cold hard lip of the toilet bowl as his lunch erupted.

"A-are you?"

"What? Hey, watch the road!"

"S-sorry." She must be losing her mind. Apologizing when he already said he was going to—she couldn't allow herself to even think the words. The sound of traffic from the opened window intensified, pushing her down to child size. How could she explain to him that she only looked like a woman, that inside she was still a frightened little girl?

Embrace me, my sweet embraceable you
Embrace me, my irreplaceable you . . .

"W-where are are you taking me?" she said.

"Where you belong."

"Oh God, please. I'll do whatever you want. Need. Whatever you say. I'll be good. Good for you. To you. Say you'll let me go then. Please, I beg you."

Sure you're a little scared, Carl baby. But you're excited too. You know you love my hands on you. My mouth and—

The sound of retching brought him back to the present.

49

"Pull over and clean it up, you pig! Take off your goddamn coat and clean it up!"

Afterward, night closed around them as they drove off into its expanse.

CHAPTER TEN

ONE morning Kate looked into the mirror, half expecting to see that her cheeks had been scarred by tears, and knew she could no longer cry. It was as though she had drained her soul. What remained was the feeling of having been torn from her moorings. She felt sore. What she and Josh referred to as "emotional flu."

But what she had to do today was too important to miss.

First, with much effort and difficulty she phoned her attorney.

"All I know, Ben, is that if everybody who got hurt by that goddamn rag sued they wouldn't be in business. What? Yes, my final word."

Toby's death had disrupted her center. Even Toby's funeral was different. If the girl had died in an accident or from some incurable disease people might have said it was God's will. But under these circumstances such words would make God seem senseless and cruel. Every phrase Kate had thought to say to Addie seemed merely to belittle the woman's loss and pain.

She dressed in a kind of fugue state caused by her long lack of sleep.

She remembered with cruel clarity going with Josh to the scene of Toby's murder. The haphazard way one leg was twisted, the congealed blood behind her little head. And Josh explaining the forensics to her with tears in his eyes. Why in hell had she gone?

"You went, Katydid," she heard her dead detective father say, "because crime scenes almost always speak of personalities."

Kate grasped the edges of the bureau and held on trying to drive her mind free of everything. She took a deep breath. It didn't help.

She felt hot, went to the bathroom and ran cold water on her wrists. Josh had taught her this athlete's trick for cooling down quickly. This did help.

At breakfast she saw blood in her pink grapefruit. She ignored the blood in her coffee, letting its warmth heighten her resolve.

Before she left the house to drive to Casey's office, Josh smiled at her, a message of courage.

The number of detectives and computers and coffee cups and litter in the large room of the task force seemed to have doubled since her last visit. The walls were covered in cork where maps of New York City had been tacked up, interspersed with photographs of women. On the maps were black x's.

As her eyes moved across the faces of the victims she saw the map of Rhinebeck. She avoided the photograph but a portrait of Toby phantomed before her. Not the Toby she had seen in the eerie light of the basement of Northern Dutchess Hospital which served as one of the county morgues. The Toby who snapped her gum and played loud music and danced, barely able to contain all the life in her.

Kate wanted to grab hold of something, shake it violently, make it shatter and break.

"Kate?"

She wheeled and saw Casey. The encouragement in his face gave her new strength. He led her to a small conference room down the hall from his office. He never strolled, but plodded.

"So?" he said when they were seated.

"That's my question."

"The girl at the perfume counter saw the victim leave with a guy who had a broken leg. About six feet, well built, handsome son of a bitch, black hair this time. Used a knife. Bite marks with his damn dental doohickey."

"And?"

"And we can't see any connection to the other victims. He leaves us nothing. Not a fiber for the spectograph. Not even spit. Heard of that guy Locarde lived in Paris in the eighteen hundreds?"

"Sure, he was the first to say that every murderer leaves something of himself at the scene."

"Yeah. I guess we just can't find it, or figure it out yet."

"Maybe. Or maybe this one leaves almost nothing behind because he doesn't have the usual subconscious wish to be caught."

"Christ on the cross! Where does that leave us? Wait for a witness of a guy's got more disguises than Lon Chaney? Or a plate number or a make on a car from a near miss?"

Near miss. The term filled her with sudden vulnerability, as if all she had were her emotions. She had been a near miss. She remembered seeing the knife flashing and believing she could see the blade as it traveled the distance between the killer and her. She had looked up from the ground where she lay, feeling as though hot soup gushed out of her belly.

"Kate?"

"Sorry."

She had shrunk into her chair. She straightened up and reached her arms around her body, as though putting herself back together.

"When, Kate?"

"I don't know. With most serial cases at some point the pace picks up. Three a year becomes six. You know. Then twice that many. We've seen the patterns. The need to kill is a drug they need more and more. Eventually the need will overwhelm him and he'll go into overdrive."

They sat quietly for a time.

"What are you thinking?" he said.

"Bothers me—why did he go to the trouble of taking Melanie Hines out of the building to kill her?"

"He must've figured if she screamed he'd be safer in the snowstorm, with no one out, than with neighbors all around in the apartments."

"Maybe . . . It only has to go down to forty degrees to snow. But to stick it's got to be thirty-two. Pretty cold for what he had planned."

"But maybe he figured if O'Rourke's girlfriend didn't see Melanie and O'Rourke back in a little while she might call the police. And if she did, and he's outside with Melanie, he's got a better shot to get away than in the apartment."

"True. But something still bothers me about this."

There was a knock on the door.

"I'm not here," Casey called out. Then to Kate: "Try to hide from detectives."

The door opened and one of the men she vaguely remembered from the cork-walled room said, "Want something to eat, Chief?"

54

"Yeah. I'd like a real Protestant sandwich. No corned beef or pastrami. No mustard. Heavy on the mayo. White bread."

She smiled, without humor.

"What about you, Kate?"

For the first time in several days she thought she might be able to muster an appetite. She wondered if the few facts she had just reviewed with Casey were responsible.

She ordered soup.

When the order-taker had left, Casey said, "How can I help you speed this up?"

She thought of Toby racing upstairs to try on her earrings.

"I want to walk through the new crime scene."

CHAPTER ELEVEN

O NE of the darkest places in the world, Kate thought, is the scene of a murder.

She stepped out of the car Casey had assigned to her and walked through the brush to where ropes marked the spot of the crime off in the distance. She switched on her tape recorder.

"You always knew who you were, didn't you? The first time was only the first time you actually did it. In your head you had already done it a hundred times, thousands.

"Everything is backward for a man like you, isn't it? Love what you hate. Pain is pleasure. Hurt is love."

Kate could see streaks of red on the winter-killed grass now.

"You always had unusual strength, didn't you? Unbelievable stamina. Comes from your anger."

She felt his bunched muscles rigid with excitement as he ordered the woman from Bloomingdale's to stop here.

"I even know why you do it. Torturing and killing is the ultimate domination, isn't it?

"I'm going to get you, you know. I made one mistake,

almost paid for it with everything I had. But I've recovered and I'm back, and I'm not going to make another.

"I know a lot about you. I know that nothing you do is an accident. Everything is part of some conscious or unconscious scheme.

"I know that you weren't born with your hatred. You had to build it carefully. First rejecting all love and affection. Then storing cruelty and neglect till it exploded. Are you terrified, too? Terrified of yourself and your power?"

An image of Toby suddenly rose in her mind, shrieking desperately and struggling with some shadowy presence, her feet sprayed in blood.

"I'll get him," she said to the dead girl. "I swear to you, honey, I'll get him."

Then she spoke to Toby's murderer again, her need to avenge the girl and Addie all-pervasive.

"I'm coming," she said, enraged. "I'm after you. For as long as it takes."

CHAPTER TWELVE

"TODAY's the day," Josh said, handing Kate a mug of breakfast tea.

Kate smiled. They hadn't seen Jenny since Toby's funeral.

She said, "She took what happened hard."

"Young. She'll bounce back. We'll all come back. How's Addie?"

"Same. She and Emmet decided to go to her sister in Florida for a while."

"Good idea."

She was grateful he didn't bring up Bermuda again, although she knew he wanted to go. She had to be here. For Toby.

They sat drinking their tea in silence for a time.

She appreciated that Josh knew that quiet was as important a part of communication as speech. Few people did.

Kate said, "Help me clear the decks before she comes?" She was trying to write again. She needed it, for balance.

"What?"

"My book."

"Shoot."

She picked up a loose-leaf folder containing her notes.

"Okay, tell me what you like best. 'People with autism don't have a clear notion of what others think, and don't know that it's different from what they think. They don't know much about people in their world so they rely on things and routines to help them cope. They don't know they have to exchange information. For example, I know one boy of fifteen whose mother repeatedly asked, 'You want to look normal, don't you?' And he would say yes. One day she asked him, 'Do you know what normal is?' 'Yes,' he said. 'It's the second button on the washing machine.' "

"*Jesus*, Kate."

"Yeah. So I keep that one in?"

"Positively. Go on."

"We're involved naturally in such a magnificent dance we don't even know we know the steps. These children need to understand things in our terms. A parent once lost her daughter near a lake and called her name at least fifty times. No response. When she found the girl the mother asked, 'Why didn't you answer?' The girl said, 'You didn't ask me a question.' "

"That's terrific, Kate!"

"You always say that."

"Want me to manufacture criticism? You're a goddamn good writer."

She put the loose-leaf folder down. "As highly functional as Lilah is . . . I was at a birthday party for one of the kids at the school the other day. She saw me but it never occurred to her to come over and chat. I said to Jenny once, 'Why are you willing to take the largest share of the responsibility in your relationship with Lilah? Lilah hardly ever thinks to ask how your life is going or what you'd prefer. When you meet it's *always* for a movie and pizza and ice cream. Doesn't that bother you?' "

"What did she say?" Josh said.

"She said, 'Lilah never lies. She's very kind if I tell her what I need and really likes having me for a friend.' "

"Too bad there's not more Jennys in this world."

"Right. It's as if these kids aren't of this culture. You say to one of them, 'Hand me the Yellow Pages, I'm very hungry,' they'll think you want to eat the phone book. We're teaching them the words without the music. What they need to know requires knowledge of culture and communication beyond language. They rely on routine. No wonder they're so good at noticing minor changes."

"That should be in your book."

She smiled. "You should be pressed in a book. How did I ever find you?"

"Lucky. More tea?"

"Thanks, no. What's the final report on the Bloomingdale's woman?"

"You promised you wouldn't today, with Jenny coming."

She looked at him in such a way that he held up his hands.

"Her vertebrae were wrenched, nerves torn, carotid paralyzed. Bastard knew how to break her neck and—"

There was the sound of a car pulling up to the house—Jenny!

"Hi!" Jenny called, walking in with a saucy bounce to her step just like her mother's.

"Hi yourself!" said Kate, smiling at the sight of the girl-woman with the guileless face and intelligent eyes.

When Jenny embraced her, Kate felt she was hugging at once niece, daughter, sister—youth itself.

After a time Kate watched as the two dearest people in her life hugged. She loved the way the girl dressed—Irish

60

sweater, and jeans so worn by wear and washing that light spilled like silk on them and they were chamois to the touch.

They had a homemade favorite meal of Jenny's, chicken pot pie and apple cobbler à la mode. Afterward Josh built a blazing fire in the den and the three of them sat watching it, delighting in each other's company.

"How's Lilah?" Jenny said.

"Terrific," said Kate.

"I just wrote her a letter."

"And the man in your life?" Josh said.

"Robbie's okay," Jenny said. Then as much to the flames as to them, "I stopped at a red light yesterday. It was next to a school and there was this teacher leading a class of kids. Toby's age. The teacher turned and looked back. She was counting like someone was missing."

Hot tears sprang from Kate's eyes. Josh pinched the bridge of his nose with thumb and index finger. The three huddled together watching dancing shapes of fire.

After a while Josh said, "How's Ginny?"

"Fine," said Jenny. Her head sagged in a way that made Kate say, "What?"

"Just that I wish everybody was as accepting as you guys. You meet this friend of mine with blue hair who wears jumpsuits of camouflage material, and you can go beyond what she seems to be."

Josh and Kate glanced at each other, ashamed of their true feelings about Ginny's appearance.

"What's wrong?" Josh said, seeing that the girl's head had sunk lower.

"I'm here to tell you it's lonely at the bottom, too."

"The bottom?" Kate said. "You?"

"Just because I don't follow everyone else. All they care about is designer names on their jeans, their shirts, their watches. It's like *they* were designed."

Josh and Kate looked into each other's faces, sharing their hurt for the girl.

"Bunch of assholes in my school."

"Let's not mince words," Josh said without anger. "But they're in my school and your aunt's, too."

Kate leaned over and kissed the girl where a wisp of her sandy hair trailed over her forehead and was lit up like a copper wire by the firelight.

Kate said, "Wish we could tell you it'll be over after college." She turned the girl around to face her. "Your mother had the same way of lifting her eyebrows when she was puzzled about something."

A smile passed over Jenny's lips.

"You're always going to feel left out because you're special," Kate added. "But there are compensations, sweetie. You'll see."

Josh placed another log on the fire then cozied in next to the women. All three watched as sparks rose and the fire blazed. They sat staring into the flames, not wanting to speak or even think lest it disturb the moment. Finally Jenny said, "I want to transfer."

Before they could react Casey called. The killer had confessed.

CHAPTER THIRTEEN

KATE waited while Josh got the parking chit. The air smelled of snow—always a talisman for her. *God let this finally be the one.* She remembered Toby's face lighting up at the sight of her and Josh's Christmas present last year.

"Looks like snow—going to be a good day," Josh said walking up to her. How delightful to have the man she loved know her so well. She could feel a smile, cautious but waiting. Still, something deep inside her was hesitant to believe the case was ending soon.

There was an excitement in the Twentieth Precinct that hummed. Kate and Josh met Casey in the captain's office. The captain escorted them to the site of the lineup. Women who had seen the killer waited outside, book-ended by detectives.

In all the lineups Kate had witnessed she never had seen so many detectives present.

Five men were brought in and directed to face front. Kate studied each one's face and posture and gait.

Nothing. Not a single vibe. Her body felt too heavy to support. Still, her instincts had been wrong before.

"Only once about serial killers, Katydid," she heard her father say. "If I had had a crap detector like yours I would of been commissioner."

When the first witness was brought in she made it known that the man third from the left was the man she'd seen. Casey slapped Kate's back and Josh squeezed her hand hopefully. The captain was beaming.

Kate studied the suspect. He was about six feet with a lean powerful build. Although he had nearly perfect features, they were forgettable as those on a billboard. Nothing of his character showed through his features.

Certainly she had interviewed serial killers in prison with similar blank expressions. Yet those killers had had an aura about them. A staticky energy. A strength they exuded. No, something more . . .

When the second witness was summoned she identified the same suspect. Josh hugged her. Casey mussed her hair. The captain shook Casey's hand.

Not just strength. Power. Adrenaline power. Not frenetic but detached. These men stood out in a crowd. It was not so much how different they appeared to others, but how, she sensed, they felt toward them. People were balloons to be pricked, food to be devoured.

The third witness agreed with the first two. Josh and Casey hugged Kate at once. Detectives came up to the captain and shook hands. Everyone in the room was smiling.

Except Kate. Trying to think of a time when her intuition had failed her in recognizing a serial killer, she couldn't.

* * *

Kate, Josh and Casey sat in the waiting room of a clinical psychologist's office. They were there to hear the test results of the confessed killer.

Josh had studied Kate as she looked at the confessor. Her face had been crumpled in anger. She was pale, and seen up close, the skin under her eyes was stained the color of coffee. Her body was younger looking now than her face.

"He's not the killer," she said suddenly.

Casey turned his scowl on her. "Not one, not two, but all three of the women make him out of the lineup as the guy they seen with his leg in a cast."

"As a guy who *could* be him," she said.

"Josh?" Casey said.

"We'll know soon enough," Josh said seeing the door to the psychologist's office open.

Dr. Aaron Norman had thinning hair and a large handlebar mustache that was compensatory.

"So, Doc?" Casey said.

Dr. Norman responded by looking at Kate when he spoke.

Psychologist to psychologist, Josh thought.

"I threw everything at him. Rorschach. Puzzle diagrams, TAT."

"Cut this shop talk." Casey said. "What's the story?" There was a sharp edge to his tone.

"The story is," Dr. Norman said, "you keep being as rude as you are, I'll put my results in the mail."

"Edgy. You know, Doc," Casey offered.

The doctor said to Kate, "The man is too out of touch with his feelings. A touch of pomposity that changes to low self-esteem for no apparent reason. He needs attention terribly. I'd say he could do with a lot of therapy."

"Doc," Casey said, "we've been waiting a long time. Is he normal?"

65

"Normal?" Dr. Norman smiled genuinely. "Was Dr. Schweitzer normal? Or how about our Presidential candidates?"

"Please, Doctor," Kate implored.

"No way this man could have committed these crimes. I'll put my reasons into my report, but I'd testify in court that he's not your man."

"How can you be so sure?" Casey said. "People are so unpredictable."

"True. But I can learn how disturbed they are, how accurate their perceptions of the world and themselves are. I couldn't say if he'd tell a bank teller he got an extra twenty-dollar bill when cashing a check. And certainly he is capable of a crime of passion, like all of us. But I know Earl Bedloe's not capable of these serial murders."

CHAPTER FOURTEEN

N ASSON stood so close to her in the convenience
store he could smell chewing gum on her breath.
Her mouth was like a gumdrop of blood. She was
disguised as a black. But he knew better: she had Her
voice.

When she looked up after gathering her candy, cigarettes and books he showed her his best smile from under
his cigar-ash-colored wig and dark glasses. Then he pretended to stumble with his bags of groceries.

"You . . . all right, mister? I mean can I help you cross
the street or something? I'm early."

A blank check for him . . .

He leaned on the cane and flashed the smile again. But
this time he made it less intense, like a fine billiard player
adjusting his English.

"You're awfully nice to help an old blind man."

"It's nothing," she said, too embarrassed by his direct-
ness to look at him.

He resisted trying to pay for her cigarettes and candy.
Like most girls, she had probably been warned to not
accept gifts from strangers.

"Why don't you let me carry those bags for you?"

Seeing his opening he said, "I'd really appreciate that. I hurt my hip last week when I fell. Think I could impose on you to help me up the steps to my room? It's only one block from here."

"Sure," she smiled and her braces glistened.

Outside the early light was alive with particles of frost that glistened in the frigid air.

Inside his room he removed his glasses. Turned the radio on loud.

"You . . . you're not blind!"

She ran to the door, where he caught her.

"What are you doing?" she said beating him with her little fists.

He was amazed at how hard she fought. How exciting her resistance was.

He couldn't allow it, though, when she began screaming. He picked up the hammer and brought it down on her again and again till she was quiet. Fit the splint inside his mouth.

Tears formed in the corners of her eyes. As he checked to see that her heart had been stilled the tears rolled down her face. He caught them with his tongue and swallowed them. Later, he would have to remember to wash off his saliva from her face.

Then he ripped off her clothes.

Who would have thought that under her loden coat with horn buttons a girl too young to drink would have such a body?

He sheared away her bra with the pruners. Then he kissed her lips. They were still warm and soft though the red circle was held with a frozen scream.

He felt the spiky tufts of hair against his cheek. Slipped on the condom.

His knees opened her unresisting legs and he forced himself into the quiet little body.

This one struggled to the very last.

Did You see how she struggled? The way I should have made You struggle, but I couldn't . . . not You . . .

He rose and maneuvered the head utilizing the opened mouth as he sometimes did. When he was finished he laid it down, closed the eyes and flushed the condom down the toilet.

Nasson smiled, feeling She had seen how many chances he was willing to take to show how he missed and needed and hated Her. Also, how brilliant he was when he had to be. Throwing them off guard, luring them in.

He washed her face to remove any trace of saliva. Then he began policing the area for the slightest traces of himself. He smiled as he heard Her again in his mind's ear, singing in a voice tinged ever so slightly with whiskey and smoke:

Embrace me, my sweet embraceable you . . .

Over and over he scoured the area. When he was certain he had not left a molecule behind he heard Her again:

> *. . . don't be a naughty baby*
> *come to Mama,*
> *come to Mama, doooo . . .*

Finally he returned to the body and inspected under her nails. There under the nail of the index finger of her right hand was *blood*. He remembered now the briefest of stabs of pain behind his shoulder when she had struggled with him. It was his blood under her nail. No doubt some of his skin, too.

He knew that with the FBI's new DNA profiling a small specimen of semen or hair or blood or saliva or skin could result in identification as accurate as fingerprints. After using condoms and the splint and shaving all his body hair, he wasn't about to let himself be identified now by what was under this one nail.

He went and got the pruning shears.

At home he enjoyed a long, slow shower and put on flannel pajamas because they felt so cozy in the winter time. He noticed that the polyethylene splint was wearing thin. He would have to construct another.

He read a book about martial arts for a while and then switched off the light.

In that state between consciousness and sleep he saw a woman's face, but he couldn't tell which one it was.

CHAPTER FIFTEEN

"**Y**ou believe how warm this winter's been?" Casey said to Josh as the doctor took a beaker of coffee from the Bunsen burner in his office/laboratory and filled their mugs. "I really think this greenhouse stuff is for real."

Josh looked at the old photograph of Jenny on his desk. She was wearing a little girl's bikini and that made him smile.

"They say it's even hotter in Europe," the Chief went on.

"Can we skip the meteorology, Case? Please? What is it?"

The Chief paused with his comedian's timing, assuming an astonished look.

"Can't I just be wanting to visit an old friend?"

"You could, but you're not. Now what?"

The pause this time was massive. Finally the Chief relented, "All right. You show two M.E.'s the same set of facts, they'll reach different conclusions, right?"

"It happens."

"You bet."

Josh saw the hard driving and heavy drinking that showed in the red flush on Casey's face and in his bluish lips. He feared that the old cop would die in two to three years, the victim of a stroke.

Casey said, "One of the nice things about growing older is losing some of your expectations, learning your limitations."

Josh studied him raptly. The bushes the detective beat around to get to his point fascinated and charmed him.

"You learn," Casey continued, "a little humility. When to ask for a little help from your friends. Now with all due respect to your old assistant, Springer, you're still the best forensic person in the world."

"Stop right there. I would never insult Jay Springer by inferring I knew one cilium more about legal medicine than he does—what the hell are you smiling about?"

"You. As usual you're always there for a friend. I already asked—no, pleaded with—Jay to do me a personal favor and beg you to take a peek at the evidence. Don't look at me like that, Josh. I told him I think he's every bit as good as you are, but sometimes a different perspective . . ."

"Jesus."

"Jay said don't worry, it'd be fun playing detective with you again."

"Jay would. And you're a conniver and a manipulator."

Casey beamed.

Josh had kissed Kate goodbye, gone to his office in Poughkeepsie.

"Morgue" was a word he considered crude and gruesome. He much preferred "mortuary" or, even better, "office." Because Dutchess County contained no separate "morgue," each hospital having in its basement a miniature one, Josh's euphemisms had become reality.

He opened his mail. There were letters from hospitals and universities, charities and foundations, former colleagues and classmates practicing all over the world. Invitations to address conferences, teaching offers from prestigious universities.

A coroner in Arizona asked about a complicated toxicological problem. Justin Rose, an old classmate, now a doctor in Belem, Brazil, sought his advice about beginning a department of forensic medicine at a local university.

"Why forensics," Justin had asked him sincerely one day, "do you have some fascination for death?"

"Cherevkoff," he had felt obliged to answer. "His legend, his intuition turned my whole world around. He let very few people get close. I couldn't believe I was one of those people. I couldn't resist learning from a genius."

The following week Justin had sent a quotation framed in teak which Josh kept on his desk:

The psychiatrist knows all and does nothing.
The surgeon knows nothing and does all.
The internist knows nothing and does nothing.
The pathologist knows everything, but a day too late.

—ANONYMOUS

Thanks to Cherevkoff, Josh knew as much as if he had been present at the deaths.

Cherevkoff. The name still stirred him, after over twenty years. A promising surgeon only in his twenties, Josh had casually attended a single lecture by the master forensic pathologist. That was all it took. He suddenly shifted to the poorly paid specialty. Cherevkoff. The master, driven by an insatiable desire for the truth at all costs. Who lived more for his work than even Casey did. The loner to the point of reclusiveness.

73

Justin Rose had again been surprised when Josh gave up his prestigious position of Chief M.E. of New York City for the ill-paid, less challenging one in Dutchess County. Especially when he could have had dozens of foundations, universities and hospitals knocking at his door.

Josh hadn't even tried to explain. Besides wanting to accommodate Kate in her desire to leave Manhattan after her near-fatal stabbing, he had found himself more and more wanting to coast. He didn't want his remaining years to go by at the speed they had as the M.E. of New York City.

He was worrying again about Kate's inability to sleep when his thoughts were interrupted by the ring of his private line.

"He got another one."

It was Casey.

"A kid this time . . . fourteen. Cut off her finger."

"Jesus. Kate know yet?"

"She wasn't home or at the Institute."

"I'll find her."

"Bastard's made it harder yet."

"Huh?"

"This one's a black."

CHAPTER SIXTEEN

K ATE said, "I brought something along I want to read to you, Case."

They were in a coffee shop two blocks from his office.

She pulled from her purse a magazine article she had clipped.

"This is about Bundy, from *Vanity Fair* this past May. Quote: There are indications that, like many serial killers, he sometimes kept the bodies as grisly trophies. Autopsies of two Bundy victims noted that, although the bodies were partially decomposed, the hair was freshly washed and fresh eye makeup had been applied. Unquote."

"Prince of a guy. What are you saying?"

"This. Quote: Among the lessons the FBI's Violent Criminal Apprehension Program unit learned from Bundy is that he returned to all his sites. Bundy told officers they might have been able to catch him if they had staked out the site after finding a body. Unquote."

"You don't want the newspapers to know about the black kid. And you want a stakeout."

She nodded.
Casey looked down into his coffee cup.
"So?" she said.
"So, you got it."

CHAPTER SEVENTEEN

WITH several ex-colleagues, Josh walked down the steel spiral staircase into the aquarium green netherworld of the Manhattan autopsy rooms. As they descended there came the gong of heavy steel doors echoing through the grotto-like, green tiled tunnels.

A gate squeaked open before them and they were in the even deeper green of the sub-basement level. The air was heavy with formaldehyde.

The group entered a gray, cold area filled with the noise of refrigerator motors cooling cadavers. There was the indecipherable garble of a PA system. A single bare bulb lighted the place and cast shadows across the walls. White tile and stainless steel. Gurney carts minus their cargo.

They walked past a wall of refrigerated compartments which ran from floor to ceiling.

Josh followed through open swinging doors and they entered a bright, white room. Here he was greeted by another set of former colleagues. Green-robed attendants with padded feet and hooded heads struck him for the first time as druidlike. Still he felt at home as he walked past pans of livers and hearts and lungs gurgling.

He looked around at the twelve tables where cadavers lay naked, flayed, their organs exposed, looking like plastic biology class models.

Pathologists were cutting, weighing, evaluating. Medical students asked questions. Police stenographers scribbled dictation from the pathologists. Behind the pathologists, dieners sewed up cadavers with black thread.

Josh followed his colleagues to the operating theater where Casey had arranged for him to give a lesson to a group of students. This lesson was being done in the spirit of camaraderie by alumnus Josh, emphasizing that his former colleagues and the current M.E. were not lacking in knowledge or technique. The media had not yet been informed of the black teenager's murder.

Soon Josh was turning down the sheet that covered the waxen cadaver. There were large contusions about the face and head. Hammer marks, he thought. Palpating the area of her neck, he could feel the fracture of the thyroid cartilage. He immediately guessed the cause of death to be an avulsion of the hyoid membrane.

"Here," he said, "the cause of death is all important."

His eyes swept up and down the length of the body taking in myriad details. Her tongue protruded and was bruised where she'd bitten during her struggle. He tucked it back in gently.

"Our bodies react to injury by mobilizing leukocytes or white blood cells at the place of injury. This can occur only in the living. The process takes from two hours to two days. In the specimens of tissue we took from this girl's body the number and type of cells tell us the wounds had been inflicted while she was alive." And after, too, he thought. He must be careful not to arouse suspicion that this was a victim of the serial murderer.

Josh screwed a jeweler's glass into his eye. The girl's eyes were still half open. With his thumb he carefully rolled the lids up revealing the widespread hemorrhage beneath.

He studied the cadaver carefully for a time, looking for some commonality that would link this girl with the other victims. To avoid arousing suspicion during the autopsy, the fingers of both hands had been clenched into fists to hide the sheared-off finger.

Josh now removed the glass from his eye and picked up one of the jewel-like dissecting knives.

"Well, ladies and gentlemen, we're ready to begin." He had already seen something.

With a nine-inch-long scalpel he made three swift incisions. Two from each tip of the scapulae, bisecting at a point straight down to the pubic symphysis. The three slashes formed a letter Y.

". . . Now with bone cutters we sever the cartilage joining ribs to sternum . . ."

Blood was seeping into the small trenches lining the table as Josh disconnected the tongue.

". . . Another stroke now severs the gullet and two or three more frees the heart and lungs. There. And there . . ."

He hauled the bloody organs out, holding them up for his audience to see.

". . . We take a sample of urine by simply pressing the bladder . . ."

He had long before seen more than enough, but continued till the procedure was complete.

What this girl and other victims had in common was little. Very little. But at least it was a beginning.

When he had washed himself and removed his greens

he trundled his way through former colleagues and assistants to the world above, First Avenue.

Kate was waiting for him eagerly when he arrived home.

CHAPTER EIGHTEEN

"**I**T'S not much of a connection," Josh said as they sat in the den. "Springer probably didn't think it of enough significance to even mention."

"What're you talking about? I don't have a hint."

"They're all smokers."

"*What?*"

"I said it wasn't much."

"No . . . I didn't understand what you meant. Cigarette smokers. Thought you were using some jargon—whatever. Hmmm, what does the connection mean to you?"

"His mother smoked? What else could it be?"

"I don't know. But maybe this connection might lead to another—Jesus, listen to me praying out loud. Am I making a complete ass of myself?"

"Complete? No."

She looked so young that he was reminded of when he first got to know her. He had felt he was meeting, so long after childhood, the perfect friend he'd longed for as a boy.

He stood and came over to her, and when she looked

into his eyes they kissed. Twenty-three years, and it was still good.

"Let's forget about all this gruesome stuff," he said. "Hang out at home. I'll make your favorite pasta sauce."

"Ronzoni, huh?"

"Ragu. And a salad, and I rented some videos on the way home. We haven't been to the movies in—"

"I love you Josh, but six strikes and you're out."

"Six?"

"Since you came home you've been playing down what you found out, trying to get my mind off things."

"That obvious?"

"That."

"So what are you planning to do about it?"

"I'm planning to take you up on your dinner offer and watch a tape after."

"That's my girl—"

"Tomorrow. Now I'm going to walk through the last scene. This time I'll be trying to feel the connection of the smoking."

CHAPTER NINETEEN

". . . ninety-nine . . . one hundred."

Nasson leaped to a standing position, aware that he had more than his usual energy for this morning's set of push-ups. He went to a window in his bedroom, opened it and took a deep breath.

The early light was alive with particles of frost that glinted in the frigid air. Just as the air had been with the last one. The one with the mouth like a gumdrop of blood. He closed his eyes and felt the spiky tufts of hair against his cheek.

Nasson was breathing heavy now with the remembrance of the scene. He lay down on the exercise mat and did three sets of a hundred sit-ups to unleash the energy. But when he'd finished his excitement had only risen.

He paced. There was nothing in the papers about finding her. And he hadn't been able to find a suitable one since. He would just go back and empty all his nerves inside her again.

But first he would need to make a new splint. Taking the stepstool from the pantry he went to the walk-in closet in his bedroom.

After he had held his calendar card against the designated spot he waited as the ceiling opened and then climbed up and sat on the cusp of the opening.

Flicking on a flashlight he took down a box labeled Press-Form Kit by Ellman Manufacturing.

In the kitchen he took one of the sheets of polyethylene and placed it in the aluminum holder. Then he sprayed the sheet with the aerosol can of pure silicone.

He heated the sheet over a portable Bunsen burner. Waited and watched for the plastic sheet to turn clear, which would prove sufficient heating.

He remembered his struggle with his need to continue biting the chosen ones without leaving incriminating saliva behind. He had decided to make an appointment with a dentist. Disguised as a housepainter, he had claimed he had a daughter who ground her teeth in her sleep.

"Why didn't you make an appointment for her?" the dentist said.

"This is kind of hard to say. I'll pay for this visit, of course, but I didn't want to bring her in if I couldn't afford it, Doc. You know teenagers and what a big deal it is for them to be embarrassed."

"Understand."

"Great. Now maybe we can get into what's best for my Marjorie."

"Not a whole lot of choice besides a dental dam. Here, let me show you."

The dentist brought out a box that might have contained handkerchiefs. Peeled off one sheet from a stack of many.

"What's it made of—latex?"

"Exactly."

"Too thin. She'll bite right through it. She's . . . schizophrenic."

"I see. Sorry. I don't think I can help you."

"Isn't there anything, some appliance you use for a different purpose that might do the trick?"

"I don't—unless . . . there *is* an occlusal splint we use after periodontal surgery."

"What's it used for?"

"Keeps food, bacteria away from the area."

"Saliva?"

"That too."

Lov-er-ly. "Can I see one?"

"I'd have to actually make one up, but I can show you the material in a kit I use."

The dentist brought out a box larger than the first. Nasson made note of the name Ellman Manufacturing.

"Isn't this polyethylene plastic?"

"Exactly."

"Could my daughter bite through that . . . I mean if she's . . . in a rage?"

"Not likely."

Nasson made note of the address in Hewlett, Long Island.

Now Nasson saw that the plastic sheet had turned clear. He took out the cement model of his teeth and upper palate. Then he took some silicone putty and pressed it down over the heated sheet he had placed over the model. He formed the sheet to the shape of the model.

As he waited the thirty seconds for the putty to cool he smiled, remembering how he had gone to Ellman Manufacturing on Long Island. Claimed to be a dentist from Milwaukee visiting friends. He'd worn bifocals, a crewcut wig and a shoe for a clubfoot. Paid cash. Let them trace that!

He popped the plastic sheet off the model. Then fitted it into his mouth.

Lov-er-ly.

85

CHAPTER TWENTY

NASSON slipped into his parka, pulled out his automatic Russian Stechkin and examined the weapon. Of all his handguns this was his favorite. Most people called anything more lethal than a water pistol an automatic. But a true automatic, which continued firing as long as you pressed the trigger, was rare. He knew of no others like the Stechkin except for an East German model used by their border guards and Russian paratroopers.

Satisfied, he jammed the pistol back into his pocket. Then he heard that terribly deep voice of Hers filled with smoke and whiskey:

> *. . . Don't be a naughty baby*
> *I love the many charms about . . .*

Nasson felt himself falling back in time. He tried with all his great strength to resist. But then he felt the power of the memory and he knew from long, painful experience when the images were this strong it was useless to fight.

He saw himself at nine standing at the top of the stairs in his parent's home.

"Carl, baby, c'mon now."

He remembered wanting yet not wanting to go down those stairs.

"C'mon, baby, come to Auntie Amanda."

Auntie Amanda who gave the most wonderful presents in the world and always took his part when Mom or Dad was scolding.

Eventually, he went down the stairs. She was in a bathrobe and when he looked into her face his heart fell. He didn't know the tone in the room had changed. He only knew he was terrified.

Yet excited. He didn't have words to put to it then but as she walked toward him he saw the whole scene as if from above his body and . . .

No! he thought, now shaking in an attempt to rid himself of the terror and left with only the excitement. Fought it with all his will. Then and now.

So, Kate thought, buckling the seat belt up and turning on the tape recorder.

"You like smokers, do you? And hate smokers?"

She swung the car out of the garage and down the driveway. The dashboard clock said 6:05. In two hours she'd be at the scene of his latest crime.

"What is it about tobacco that turns you around and drives you? A woman, isn't it? A woman who smoked cigarettes. Was it your mother? I know it's not the nicotine, is it?"

Up and down the sides and corners of her mind an intuition was changing into noise.

7:35 P.M.

As the taxi sped along FDR Drive downtown Nasson looked out the window at the ice floating on the Harlem River.

When he heard Her voice he cracked the window and for a short while he was aware of only the wind sound.

But then Her voice prevailed.

. . . I want my arms about you . . .

He leaned over the open window, gulping draughts of air. But was only filled with the old familiar formula of fear and excitement.

. . . My sweet embraceable you . . .

7:30 P.M.

As Kate swung her car off the Willis Avenue Bridge and headed for FDR Drive she heard her father's voice.

"Learn to read a room, Katie. Look for what they place at eye level where they can always see it."

"What about if you don't know where they live, Pop?"

"Work with what you got. There's always something. All these women being smokers, for instance."

"What do you make of that?"

"Same as you. His mama smoked."

"Not enough."

"Maybe she burned him with her cigarettes when he was real little. What is it, Katie?"

"I have this feeling . . . like there's something very obvious I'm not seeing."

Silence surrounded them. But she knew he would feel it.

"Never underestimate intuition," he said.

It was a tenet of her profession to wait for the truth to emerge rather than to prod it.

"We'll see," she said.

She felt his absence, his voice replaced by the high speed wail of cars on the drive. She yearned to see once more his generous and rhythmic old beat cop's walk.

7:51

Nasson stepped out of the taxi in front of the same convenience store where he had met the last one and walked toward the furnished room. He had paid two months in advance so there was no need for the landlady to have stopped by. If the papers hadn't carried anything about the last one, he was safe.

And when she was discovered the landlady would tell the police that the room had been rented by a blind old man.

As he neared the building where the furnished room was he reached into his coat. One whole pocket was almost taken up by the automatic.

Then he heard Her voice. Even if he became deaf he would still hear Her. He gripped the gun handle as the building came into view.

8:02

Kate stuck the parking lot chit into her purse and headed toward the corner. There she waited in front of a convenience store till the light turned red.

When she saw the building she was suddenly struck by the conviction that the killer was coiled nearby.

She could feel his cunning, his power. Most of all, his madness.

She gulped great breaths of air, fighting dizziness. She remembered that moment, years earlier, when she'd realized she was knifed. Leaning against a wall, she saw the flash of the blade. Felt her blood ooze from her again. Smelled her own death.

Was he here? How close?

She fought with the same determination she had then to prevent herself from passing out, as though giving in to unconsciousness would be fatal now, as then. Began to breathe more easily.

Maybe he wasn't here. She was just spooky. Dreading the kill scene because of all it would bring back to her.

Determined, she moved on down the street.

8:05

What Nasson saw made him feel his eyes were growing. In the light of the vapor lamp way down the street stood the woman who had called him a lying ten-year-old.

He felt her neck between his hands, saw terror in her eyes. *Cunt.*

At this very moment he might be in the sight of some detective on stakeout.

He froze for seconds before he adjusted the expression on his face and said to himself, *I am calm. I'm squeezing the handle of my weapon. I AM DEADLY.*

He swung round, searching for a man in a parked car.

He tried to formulate theories and conclusions. Why had the police kept the story out of the papers? He was filled with a rage that suffused his entire being. It felt as if the night were alive about him. He needed revenge. And not with his automatic or a knife. Nothing less direct than his own hands could tear the rage from him.

CHAPTER TWENTY-ONE

KATE fished tissues from her purse and patted her forehead dry. Her palms were wet. She had always been ashamed that her hands were not graceful like her mother's but short and thick like her father's. Now she took comfort in them and imagined feeling her hand on his. Such a cushioned squeeze he'd had, with a padding of fat, but underneath, his bone and muscle were like metal pushing through foam rubber.

Easy, she said to herself. Usually conjuring up thoughts of her father helped to contain fear.

She pictured the killer's hands violating the young black victim's skin. She shuddered.

Nasson wheeled and darted around the corner of the building. A pulse pounded between his eyes.

Collect yourself. Think. There could be a cop inside.

He felt a rush of rage against her and fought to hold it back while he decided what to do next. But the rage grew till he yearned again to have his hands on her neck or her throat. He dreamt of ways he could make her suffer: The hammerlock that cracked a spine, the reverse pressure of two hands that broke the neck.

A cold rain began to fall making the air smell of iron and cement. Under a street lamp that threw off light defiantly, she hesitated.

"Going out?" she heard a streetwalker ask a middle-aged man.

A homeless person was relieving himself in a storefront. When he turned, his underlip, red as a worm, pushed out of his beard. Dirt was so ground into him that it occurred to her it probably couldn't even be scraped off.

In the country she rarely saw eyes so devoid of mercy, mouths so scornful, jaws so lax with hopelessness. Who would help her here if he came at her? Casey had said he would station a man nearby, but would he be a match for Nasson? She remembered the enormous shape of Frank O'Rourke, his head split open like a melon, on a street like this. Saw Melanie Hines' blood staining the entire back seat of the parked automobile on such a street.

She hadn't left Josh and driven two hours at night to turn back now. She crossed the street, heading toward the building.

As soon as she entered the hallway which smelled of cat urine she could feel the force of his concentration. A wave of cold rose from her feet. After she had been stabbed she had kept a gun on her nightstand for months, carried it into restaurants, into the library. How she wished she had the weapon now.

She came to the door Casey had told her to look for. Using the key he had given her she unlocked the door and went inside. Found a light switch, flicked it on.

There was blood on the carpet. The killer had been

there not long ago. Some of his breath would still be in the air.

She imagined what he had looked like to the young black victim. Eyes which did not see her as human. Mouth grotesquely distorted by his appliance. Gloved hands. Shivering, she felt an odd warmth. Turned on her tape recorder.

"Did Mom burn you with her cigarettes? Were there always overflowing ashtrays around her when you were growing up?"

She recognized a familiar aching in her armpits where the adrenal glands were straining.

A new kind of energy boiled in Nasson. His pupils were so enlarged with rage he saw out of focus. To make her suffer, he could shoot her in the stomach. It was a slow, painful way to die. The liver, pancreas, kidney, and stomach walls broke, but the heart kept getting blood. Took a long time to go into a coma.

"What did you experience the first time, so that you had to have more? The thrill of realizing you'd been in great jeopardy? The kind of fear that makes nightmares? But it was also like being electrified, wasn't it? Seductive fear. It was addictive—right?"

A set of books on the floor. She knelt down, saw they were schoolbooks. She thought of Toby, saw the haphazard way one of the girl's legs had been twisted, the congealed blood at the back of her head. If he had done that to Toby, what would he do to her?

"You've learned to be a lot more careful than you were the first time? Haven't you?"

93

One of the books was a grammar text Jenny had used as a child.

"It's rage makes you do it, isn't it? Out-of-control hatred for certain women who remind you of her. Of Mom. Like all the different parts of you are at war."

As she crept toward the unexplored bedroom, fear made a huge bubble push up in her chest.

Kate entered the bedroom, saw the smashed lamp, the blood on the ravaged sheets and pillows. She had never seen fury so potent, so unbridled. Shrill screams were latent in the air. She thought she would be sick. She planted her hands against the wall for support. The wall felt slick and gelatinous—or was it her palms? Her hands slipped on it. It seemed to her she became huge and vulnerable, naked, phosphorescent to some watching eyes.

His eyes. Filled with fury. Merciless.

Hurrying now, Nasson said to the lying criminologist cunt in his thoughts, "I'm going to tie you up. Then slowly drop acid into your spying eyes. You're going to watch the liquid moving slowly to the bottle's lip. See the first drop trembling slightly, reluctant to fall from the glass. Then falling toward you. See how well you can spy on me then."

Kate heard a creaking sound from the entrance of the apartment. Filled with the conviction that the killer was present, she could feel her scalp tighten and her hairs seemed to separate with alarm.

She saw the streaks of red on the winter-killed grass where he had tortured the woman from Bloomingdale's. Felt his muscles bunch with excitement as he stalked the woman, watched her. Felt his exhilaration. His rage. His precision.

Then she pictured his shape, rain-soaked, gleaming and sharp as a knife, filling the doorway. Saw the hammer in his right hand being raised as he swooped down on her. She froze in sudden and complete terror.

She jumped backward and suddenly realized none of this was happening. She let out what little breath was left in her.

Her knees buckled, reacting to tension, and she sat down hard, staring at her legs as if they were betrayers.

Without warning, the lights went out.

Mother of God.

She clapped a hand over her mouth. Squeezed her eyes shut, expecting a blow.

Footsteps. Heavy ones. Getting closer. Her bladder filled. This time it wasn't her imagination.

She blinked her eyes open. Beam of a flashlight approaching. She searched desperately in the dark for a weapon. Clutched a book. Hail Mary, fullofgrace, fullofgrace, fullofgrace.

She had survived the last killer. Would she this time? She trembled feeling his sense of invincibility, his remorselessness, the inhuman strength his rage gave him.

The undeniably large, meaty paw of a man gripped her shoulder.

He had found her.

She was blinded by the light.

CHAPTER TWENTY-TWO

THROUGH his recently unfocused eyes Nasson saw the brown out cause the lights to go out on the street, including the building the spying bitch was in. Saw what must be the super's flashlight searching for the source of the problem.

He decided to wait for a better opportunity. But he had to wait for over an hour before he was calm enough to leave.

He didn't go home. Obviously they had a purpose for keeping the discovery of the latest out of the news. Probably hoped he would return, too.

To be extra safe he would establish another identity. He was prepared, having already researched the matter in the library. He had always been able to find in books everything he needed to know to carry out his missions. He knew all the procedures, from procuring a social security number, to acquiring a post office box, to establishing an address for himself. Also a bank account and a couple of credit cards which he used just enough to keep them active. Simultaneously he would establish credit and obtain his new name and social security number. Then, with the help of a good copying machine, he'd doctor his real birth certificate to give it his new name.

Finally, he'd present the dog-eared copy, along with his new identification at a local post office. In a couple of weeks he'd receive a brand new U.S. passport in his new name. No fake or forgery to trace.

This time, though, he would not only change his name and the way he looked, he would change his sex.

He was ready. He had already found a publication called *The Transvestian* which listed places where a "TV" could buy dresses, shoes, blouses, bags, wigs and cosmetics. He had also answered an ad for those wanting to learn how to use makeup like a woman.

In the morning he would buy clothes and makeup and wigs. Then he would go to the public library at Fifth Avenue and Forty-Second Street and find out all he could about the spying bitch and her husband.

Nasson dropped to the floor and began doing push-ups. He would work out till he had dissipated enough anger so he could think and plan calmly. Sleep. A man with all that he had to do needed rest and strength.

"Here you are, Red," the middle-aged cab driver said, pulling up to the library.

Nasson smiled at his successful disguise.

"Hey, you aren't one of those spitfires, are you? Built like Maureen O'Hara, too."

He continued to smile though the man was making him sick. Never knew what the police could do with a seemingly unconnected lead—like a redheaded woman breaking a cabbie's nose.

The main reading room was filled with scholars. A few homeless people dozed in their seats. He went to where copies of the *Times* were on fiche and set to work. He expected to spend hours but in less than thirty minutes he found what he wanted buried on page eleven of a recent edition:

Former chief medical examiner of New York City, Joshua Berman, performed an autopsy for students of forensic medicine at the request of current medical examiner Jay Springer.

Nasson looked at the date of the newspaper. Six days ago. The very next day after he had chosen the last one.

He was tempted to spend the remaining part of the day researching the spy and her husband, to see how best to hurt them. But first he would pay a visit to the Manhattan morgue to see what games they were up to.

"Yes, can I help you?" said a security guard with goiterous eyeballs.

"Please excuse my voice," Nasson whispered, holding a lace handkerchief with his wrapped-nail fingers. "Bad laryngitis." Slowly, deliberately, he took a cough drop from his purse and popped it into his mouth.

"Yeah?" the guard said.

"I'm from the new magazine, *True Medicine*. We'd like to do a piece on the morgue."

"Have to talk to Miss Stoddard, Director of Public Affairs. Have a seat. Name?"

"Darla Lagno."

It was one thing having a taxi driver and a security guard believe he was a woman, another to fool a real woman.

He examined the waiting room's blue-tiled floor, large house plants that framed picture windows and row of chairs backed up against a wall. Not very ominous. Not inviting either. He was trying to decipher the Latin words on the marble wall to his left when a woman's voice interrupted.

"Miss Lagno?"

The dress and shoes seemed more the choice of an older woman than the thirtyish one who stood before him, but her posture and the fit of her clothes indicated poise and taste.

Nasson took the woman's hand limply. "Please," he whispered. "My voice . . . laryngitis." He took out another cough drop and slipped it daintily into his mouth.

"Doctor told me whispering is the worst thing you can do with laryngitis."

Nasson nodded, forcing a smile. "Can't help it," he whispered back.

"Do you have identification?"

He fished out of his purse the press card he had forged.

Miss Stoddard looked it over and handed it back saying, "Doug said you wanted a tour. We can't allow anyone below till all the autopsies are over. Invasion of privacy."

"Understood." Then, to take possible suspicion away from his disguise, he pulled a notepad and a pen from his purse saying, "The Latin words, what do they mean?"

" 'Let conversation cease. Let laughter flee. This is the place where death delights to help the living.' "

Nasson looked up from his note taking. "Very interesting."

"Was there anything specific you wanted to know?"

"A Dr. Joshua Berman gave a guest lesson last week. Isn't that unusual?"

A darkness passed over Miss Stoddard's face.

"Yes, it is unusual. But the current medical examiner and J—uh . . . Dr. Berman . . . are old friends. Perhaps you'd like to speak to one of the detectives?"

"That won't be necessary," he rasped.

"They're right here, around the corner."

"Really . . ." Nasson said, coughing.

"No trouble. We've got detectives here from each borough."

He felt a cold, numb spot the size of a silver dollar form on his forehead. Calm and deadly, that's what he was.

Miss Stoddard ushered him into an office. He was introduced to a detective who looked chronically suspicious, despite his boyish features.

After Miss Stoddard had gone Nasson opened his purse, pretending to be searching for something, holding the automatic.

"So?" the detective said. "What can I do for you?"

"We . . ." he whispered, "my editor, that is, saw that Dr. Berman was here last week for a guest autopsy, you might say." He paused here expecting a chuckle. There was none. Outside there was the *whoop* of an ambulance's siren. "He—"

"Who?"

"My editor."

"Yeah, right."

Doubt made the detective's eyebrows rise.

Perhaps Stoddard and the detective who sat before him had been warned to suspect anyone asking about the autopsy. But it was too late. To switch to another topic now would be suspicious. Offense was the best approach.

"I'll level with you, detective," he whispered. "We've gotten reports that the young black girl Dr.—"

"How'd you know about that?"

Bingo!

"You know as press we can't divulge our sources."

"You mean you won't."

"I didn't say that."

"Never mind. So?"

Now to get this moron onto other things. "So we heard,

and this is only rumor, mind you, that Dr. Berman may be coming back to replace Dr. Springer, who's ailing."

The detective shook his head, relieved.

"All due respect, I won't even give these rumors any uh . . ."

Credence, you fool.

". . . any kind of, ah, weight by answering. No offense, lady, but this ain't no coffee klatch or fishing expedition."

Nasson bit back a smile and rose from his seat.

"Sorry to have troubled you, officer." Coughed.

"No trouble at all."

In the street the odor of low tide steaming out of the sewers matched the foul taste in his mouth. Berman would pay for all the shit he'd been taking, and for the cramp in his instep from having to wear women's shoes. Berman and his spying cunt of a wife and his whole fucking family.

Killing the Bermans was too mild a retribution.

An idea struck him. Instead of going straight home and unhitching himself from these bindings and straps he would first return to the library.

He allowed his hate to boil to the surface.

CHAPTER TWENTY-THREE

"**G**REAT night for comets. New moon, dark skies," Kate said, entering Josh's observatory.

Josh moved away from his telescope, smiling. "Didn't mean to disturb you."

"Disturb, disturb. I was missing you."

She didn't know what she liked more, his deep, soft voice with its rough old-fashioned New York accent or his kind words. She looked around for a place to sit. Here Josh lived in clutter, as if it were important to leave his mind liberated and the surroundings messy. She decided to stand.

"How you doing?" he said, coming up and brushing a stray lock from her forehead.

The unrelenting dark drizzle of fear had at last subsided since that night at the last crime scene, when she had turned and seen that the hand gripping her shoulder belonged to a building superintendent. For the first time in over two weeks she realized she could truly be present for him.

"It's pretty much over, isn't it?" he said.

"How did you know?"

102

"The way you slept last night. Your voice is even different."

No one had ever known her as well as he. She studied him. He was like some giant, middle-aged sea captain whose many voyages had toughened him for the worst without making him cynical.

She said, "Thanks for how you've been these—"

"Shhh." He loved breathing the same air as she when she slept. Food tasted better when prepared with her hands. He had never thought of himself as a lucky person till she entered his life.

"Before I came over here," she said, "I was thinking, when we first met you used to say we lived like we were on a star. Must've been lonely for you on that star lately."

He smiled tenderly. "Wasn't very long."

"Started way before this last incident. When Toby got killed. Different from lately, but still, I wasn't available to you."

"Kate—"

"No, let me finish, honey. Please. I want to go back to that star again with you."

He took her gently by her shoulders and looked directly into her eyes. He noticed that etched around them were those first lines which made her more real to him than ever. "We never left that star."

"I don't know what I ever saw in you . . ."

"Likewise."

"I'm going to keep working on this case. But back to our star."

They sat on a convertible couch from their first apartment which neither could part with.

She took his hair in both hands and let it sift through her fingers slowly. It felt so good he wasn't able to move. He leaned his head back and she held it in her hands.

103

After a time he said, "I really enjoy having you back."

"So, is that as close as you're going to get?"

Smiling, he stood with her and pulled out the couch so it became, once again, their first bed.

CHAPTER TWENTY-FOUR

T HE following morning after seeing Lilah Kate wrote:

Because children with autism live in a confusing world they have a dependence on routine and objects. Some go through a phase where they carry round their favorite things and become quite despondent if they're lost.

Some become frightened of harmless things because of isolated incidents. One boy who had reached into a too hot bath refused to bathe again for a year. A girl who had had her heels rubbed by a new pair of shoes thereafter insisted on remaining barefoot.

The phone rang. It was Marsha Clark, returning Kate's phone call. Marsha was in charge of Valeur, the former Astor-Prince Obolensky Mansion in Rhinebeck which now had catering facilities.

"My husband's fiftieth birthday is in a little more than two weeks. Is that Saturday available? I know it's short notice."

When Marsha asked her to hold Kate smiled, thinking about her breakfast conversation with Josh:

"So," she had said, "how does it feel, fifty?"

It was as though he were waiting to be turned on.

"Do you realize I was born before television, credit cards, Xerox, contact lenses, penicillin and the Pill?"

"I see you haven't given this much thought. What else?"

"There were no pantyhose, women wore nylons. People got married first and then they lived together."

She laughed loudly.

"Closets were for clothes, not for coming out of. The only guys who wore earrings were pirates in the movies. 'Made in Japan' meant junk."

"Got the point. What's it like for you now?"

"Now, especially in the city, I'm often the oldest person in a restaurant, the movie theater, sometimes even the whole damn airline terminal. I got off the wrong floor in Macy's last month. There was a young couple in their twenties buying a sofa together. They were holding hands. I found myself watching them like an old guy on a park bench looking at the young ones."

"What do you want to do on your birthday?"

"City Island for dinner, sit looking at the water drinking wine and eating lobster over linguine."

She smiled. It was where he had asked her to marry him. "Watching the water in December?"

"So we'll watch the icebergs."

"We do have a Saturday available because of a cancellation, Dr. Berman . . ."

"What? Oh," she said into the receiver. "Sorry, Marsha. Daydreaming. Please call me Kate. That would be terrific. Are you free at all today? I'd like to discuss it."

After making an appointment for forty minutes later, Kate returned to her writing.

Autism is a disability which lasts all through life.
Adults with autism have shown they can work at ordinary

jobs and live out their lives in their communities . . . But most will need considerable support. Job coaches are sorely needed, as are group and satellite homes and apartments for those who no longer have families with whom they can live. Very little has been done anywhere in this country to provide these services.

It is our responsibility to protect their dignity and allow them to have the shape of their own souls.

The manner in which a society treats its most vulnerable citizens is one index by which it is judged by other nations and history.

Kate looked at her watch, set her pen down, excitement over Josh's party arrangements mounting in her.

She left the house happy about her talk with Josh.

Nasson crouched in the woods nearby. He set his binoculars down and folded up the parabolic microphone.

CHAPTER TWENTY-FIVE

.

"**W**HATEVER happened with the landlady who rented the room where he killed the black school kid?" Casey said.

It was nine A.M. Monday. Briefing. Dozens of detectives looked down into their working notebooks.

A voice called back, "He paid her in cash. No I.D. This time he was disguised as an old blind guy. Bad lead."

"I'm sick and tired of this bad lead, no lead bullshit. Make a lead, goddamit. Check everybody who works in the building. Maybe someone else saw something the woman missed. Got it?"

"Sure, Chief."

"Well, get it done. I don't care how many people it takes. I'll break some out of uniform, I have to. So far I got a million pages of reports don't mean shit. I'm under pressure and it's going to get worse. There'll be media people who'll want to talk to you individually—no way. What about this contraption he uses in his mouth?"

"There's a hundred eighty-three thousand dentists in the country," a detective called from the back of the room.

Casey said, "Start with New York State, Seager."

"There's thirteen thousand one hundred eighty in the state. You got your periodontists, your ortho—"

"Who cares how they're broken down. Do them all."

"But Chief, according to my sources there's more than one way to make something to hold back the saliva. You got your vacuum machine and this splint you make from—"

"What are you—the freaking tooth fairy?"

There were scattered guffaws.

"Check it out. All out. Period. What about the days of the week he does it—any pattern?"

"None," another detective answered. "Weekdays, weekends, morning, afternoon, night."

Casey said, "Any days he skipped?"

"A few Tuesdays and a Thursday," someone yelled.

"Keep a watch on it. What about intervals between?"

"No pattern, Chief," said an Asian detective. "Except the time is getting shorter."

"That's the pattern with these serial guys, Zhang," Casey said. "In time he'll need to do it more and more and he won't be so careful."

"But he may be picking them out months in advance," said a woman detective.

"That's encouraging, Kelsey," Casey said sarcastically.

"I didn't mean—"

"I know what you meant. You're right."

"He leaves us nothing," Detective Kelsey went on. "The only pattern here seems to be that they're all women. And they're all smokers."

Casey slammed his fist down on the table. "I'm not going to listen to that kind of bullshit answer anymore. It's not just an answer, it's an attitude. Sure as Mother Teresa shits in the woods, there's always a pattern. We just got to find it. A copy of every interview, every lead, every single piece of paper generated by each and every one of you every day gets put into the file. Everyone reads that file every night.

"People are panicking. Soon you'll have a kid come home from college at night when the family don't expect him and his father blowing him away with the family gun.

"Anybody gets an idea in between briefings call me. All vacations and days off are canceled till we stop this dirtbag."

"My husband's going to be crazy about this," Kelsey said under her breath.

"Screw your husband," Casey said without anger.

"*When?*" she answered.

The room exploded with laughter.

Casey smiled, "Very funny. All right, settle down. The cholesterol and carcinogens are on me today. You, Kelsey, with the horny husband, take the order."

CHAPTER TWENTY-SIX

NASSON shut off the ignition in the Valeur parking lot. He had chosen to buy a mid-sized, powder blue 1976 Chevrolet because he knew mid-seventies GM cars like this were so plain and unassuming no one was likely to notice them. Generic was the word he liked to use. Even a Detroiter with an interest in the auto industry might be hard pressed to make a positive identification on such an invisible car.

He checked his disguise in the rear view mirror. For aging he had exaggerated the areas of his face where he guessed deep lines would appear in ten or twenty years. Then, working with a light hand, he had shaded lines in with soft eye shadow pencil in a brown shade. He had blended in the color so carefully that not even the merest indications remained. He also applied blue-gray eye shadow subtly into the under-eye area, and a blush darker than his normal color to create the illusion of ascetic sunken cheeks and temples. He left his shaved head bare.

Dressed in a camel coat, jeans and beige corduroy blazer, Nasson made one last adjustment to the brown knit tie which he wore over his blue denim shirt.

He made his way to the mansion, where a Russian coat of arms hung outside the front door.

While he waited in the center hall for the manager, Nasson took note of the large sofas and chairs, some Victorian, others French Provincial and Contemporary. Everywhere there were Oriental carpets, great brass chandeliers, sconces and medieval tapestries.

"Miss Clark will see you now," said the young man who had introduced himself earlier as "one of the caretakers."

Nasson was led to an office where every available table was crowded with framed bridal photographs.

"She'll be right with you," the young man said, and left.

Immediately Nasson sprang to a desk in a corner of the room. Spied a leather calendar book and opened it. Flipped through to today's date and saw a notation for an earlier appointment with Kate Berman. Turning the pages quickly he stopped when he found:

Birthday Party	*Josh Berman*
7 PM hors d'oeuvres	*Ferncliff Room*
8 PM Dinner	*Astor Salon*
50 people	*Caterer Cordon Bleu*

Nasson heard the unmistakable sound of a women's heels in the corridor outside, and hurried back to his seat.

Marsha Clark had a bearing at once authoritative and feminine, and with the kind of trim, vivacious good looks that made it difficult to tell her age. Nasson guessed in her mid-thirties.

"Thank you for seeing me," he said. "My name is Lyman Masters. I'm writing a book about the greater mansions in Dutchess County. Vanderbilt, Mills, Château de Montgomery. I wonder if you'd be kind enough to have someone show me around?"

"I'll do better than that. Follow me."

As he followed and listened to her speak, Nasson took a notepad and pen from his pocket. While pretending to make notes he was sketching a map of the place.

". . . When John Astor died on the *Titanic* his son inherited the mansion and then . . ."

Eight minutes later Nasson was shown the Astor Salon where the Berman party would be held.

"Lovely tapestries, and I adore the fireplaces and the brass chandeliers. You've certainly kept the integrity of the place."

"Thanks. Come on, we'll do upstairs now."

He followed her up a long flight of maroon carpeted stairs.

"The patina on these old wooden banisters is particularly gorgeous," he said.

"I'm glad you like them."

At the top of the landing they walked through an arched entryway. To the left there was a powder room.

"Tell me," he said. "Are there any secret passageways or rooms? People love to read about that sort of thing."

"No, but if you give me a minute . . ." She pointed to a locked door to the right of the powder room. "I'll take you behind this locked door to a stairway that leads out to the rear of the mansion."

"Terrific."

While he waited he examined the door lock. A second or two with the pick gun he'd modified in size and quietness and he'd have it open.

"Now," said the manager, returning with a key, "follow me."

Behind the door was a spiral staircase that led down.

113

Nasson could hardly contain his excitement as they descended it.

At the foot of the staircase was a huge door. He watched as she took a key from a hook next to the door, unlocked and swung it open.

He followed her up the stairs and outside into the cold afternoon.

"The rear of the mansion," he said.

"Exactly."

Nasson grunted. He would park his car here. Then, somehow—he would need a plan—he would be waiting for her when she came out of the bathroom. Tell her there's a gun in her back and force her down the spiral steps and into the car and away.

He'd pay anything to see the expressions on the Bermans' faces when they realized their precious niece was gone.

Now all he had to figure out was how to crash the party and get close enough to Jenny dear.

CHAPTER TWENTY-SEVEN

NASSON was eager to deliver his punishment to the Bermans on the night of their party, but he was grateful for the intervening weeks which would allow him to perfect his plan.

Posing as a retired professor of drama he leased a brownstone in the Village in Manhattan. The owners were a retired couple who would be traveling for at least six months, maybe longer. He wouldn't have to deal with their mail or with people dropping in.

Working alone, he began to construct a studio in an apartment of the house. He chose a bedroom which had an adjoining toilet, removed the doors and moldings. Added soundproofing, then Sheetrock. Designed a set of shelves so that hinges and lines were concealed. The entire set was built so that it would slide.

He made his access entrance swing into the secret space to make construction easier and eliminate the need for invisible hinges. This also removed the possibility of telltale scrapings on carpet and floor.

For the mission ahead he would have to be perfect in his woman's disguise. He began to frequent a bar that catered to transvestites, and studied their ways.

From a particularly feminine sounding gay transvestite called Janine, he learned how, with concentration, he could change the pitch of his voice to higher than normal. To change the harmonies caused by resonances within the throat or the mouth was more difficult. He learned where to shop for a false palate. Finally, he found one with just the right thickness. The combined effect of the higher pitch and softer resonance gave a distinctly womanish flavor to his voice.

He discovered how to more effectively remove facial and body hair by waxing rather than shaving. His skin was sensitive to the process but he treated it with refined, odorless olive oil. As the days passed his skin adapted to the treatments.

He cut down to a thousand calories a day.

He studied the newspaper files at the Forty-Second Street library and compiled a thorough knowledge and history of the Bermans and their niece.

By the day of the party, Nasson had lost sixteen and a quarter pounds. He had arranged to have Janine help him achieve a perfect disguise. She recommended he be a brunette, because it was the coloring which attracted least attention. Together they had purchased a lace-backed human hair piece from one of the best wig shops in the city. Dyed Nasson's eyebrows to match. Wrapped, manicured and creamed his hands and feet.

Now, in her apartment on Barrow Street, Janine applied the finishing makeup touches, then slipped the black dress over Nasson's slim hips. Both looked into the full-length mirror.

Nasson smiled at the precision of their work. He liked precision. *Do You see how brilliant I can be?*

"So-o-o, baby," Janine said, "are you gorgi or not?"

Nasson took a step backward for leverage and in one

silken motion spun Janine round and rabbit-punched the back of his neck, breaking it.

He had liked Janine, but anonymity was his prime concern.

Nasson slipped into his fur, picked up his evening bag, adjusted his pearls and left for the party.

CHAPTER TWENTY-EIGHT

A s Nasson approached the mansion through its stone pillars and drove the half-mile entrance road lined with cedar, and locust bereft of their leaves, he could feel excitement rise between his legs.

Almost immediately after he entered the central hall of the mansion an egg-shaped man approached.

"Can I get you a drink, dear?" the man said in a bicycle horn voice, eyes flirtatious.

"Maybe later," he said, and saw that the fool had actually *liked* his voice and his looks.

Nasson followed a black waitress carrying a tray of baked Brie with melon balls to an open bar where a line had already formed.

The Bermans were nowhere to be seen.

He wanted a Rob Roy but ordered a Perrier and lime. He would keep his senses and coordination keen while not appearing conspicuous without a drink.

Corks popped, glasses clinked, people laughed.

He spied Casey at the bar. Last night CBS had run an editorial calling for the Commissioner's resignation. That, he thought with glee, must have lit a flame under Casey the size of Mount St. Helens.

The detective looked his way and Nasson delighted in locking gazes with the blind fool.

"Blinis and caviar?" He turned and saw the egg-shaped man offer a miniature plate.

"Thanks, no, I'm waiting for someone," he said, fingering the automatic through his sequined evening bag.

The man left just as the volume in the room increased.

Nasson turned and smiled as he saw the Bermans and their niece entering the area. The hate rose up and he told himself, Soon, now.

Hugs, kisses, scattered applause.

Nasson was pleased to see how happy all three were. It would make what he was going to do even more devastating.

He drifted closer to the threesome. Josh Berman had the kind of face that reveals everything at once. So happy. So sure of the future. So in for the shock of his fucking smug life.

These two, without provocation, had been conspiring against him for months. Now they didn't know that he was standing less than ten feet away, sipping their Perrier. Delighted, he wanted to laugh out loud. "It's me," he wanted to shout. "Here, look over here. I'm the one."

"To the birthday boy," someone shouted, and the scene was filled with raised glasses directed at the medical examiner.

Nasson drifted closer, watching the Bermans nod and hug and kiss the well-wishers clustered around them.

He was so close now he could see the faint down on their precious niece's upper lip.

At a certain point Kate Berman, rushing over to hug a woman, passed so close that Nasson could feel the heat of her body radiating from her. When she turned, arm in

119

arm with the woman, the elbow of her right arm brushed his shoulder. The feeling was exquisite. He had to concentrate on his breathing to contain his excitement and anticipation.

Not wanting to appear unusual, he accepted a waitress's offer of crudité with *aioli* and herb dip. He bit daintily into a floret of broccoli.

He looked at his lady's Cartier watch: 7:35! By eight, dinner would be served and his plan would be ruined.

After getting another Perrier he began to walk toward the threesome. Picked up his speed. Just as he drew alongside the niece, he pretended to trip, deliberately spilling Perrier on her.

All six Berman eyes fastened on him. It was too giddy and unreal to believe.

"I'm *so* sorry, dear," he said, offering a lace hanky. "Here, it's only Perrier. Not to worry."

"No problem," the niece said. She smelled of vanilla and clean cloth.

"Let's go to the ladies' room," Kate Berman said.

"You stay with your guests," the girl answered, "I'll go."

"Let me help you, dear," Nasson said, thinking how they would remember this moment later. He took the girl's arm and led her away. "Happy birthday," he shouted over his bare shoulder. "The bathroom upstairs is less crowded," he cajoled.

"Great."

As the pair ascended the maroon carpeted stairs Josh turned to Kate, "Woman looked like a road company Jane Russell."

"Boy, are you showing your age."

"Who do you think brought her?"

"Probably Robert Mitchum."

Josh smiled. This evening, before getting dressed, he had gone to his observatory. Orion had hung off in the west and the rising of the Pleiades was in the east. The rising of the Pleiades was always a good omen for him. How lucky he was to have Kate and Jenny and all these wonderful friends.

Without warning Kate found her heart thrusting against her ribs. She could hardly breathe.

She excused herself and went outside to sort out her feelings. Since the party began she had had a general feeling of uneasiness and disorientation without any facts to justify it. She shook her head. She must be wrong. Undoubtedly the accumulation of stress.

She took some deep breaths and went inside.

Nasson led the niece into the bathroom.

"It's really nothing," the girl said.

She had soft brown eyes. Her left pupil showed a tiny wedge of yellow, as if warning of her vulnerability.

"I'll wait outside for you, then," Nasson said and left.

Outside he took his miniature pick gun from his bag. As he had practiced at home, he stood with his back to the locked door, found the keyhole, set the pick in and activated it. He could feel when the pick snapped up and hit the bottom pin, bouncing the top pin out of the cylinder and into the shell. As he applied light turning pressure with the tension wrench, the top pins were caught in the shell and the cylinder turned.

He had just replaced the pick gun inside his bag when the niece reappeared.

"All set?" Nasson said moving up to her.

In that instant Jenny saw that the whole of the stranger's face was smiling fixedly, except for the eyes which were doing something else entirely. There was something brutal in that look.

Suddenly a hand as big as a baseball glove appeared over her face. Its touch made her bowel turn. Another hand, no, a finger, dug in behind her left ear.

121

Nasson released his finger from the girl's nerve, satisfied that she was unconscious.

Holding her up, so he would seem to be helping a drunk if seen, he pushed the unlocked door open with his knee and disappeared with the girl behind it.

7:58

In a little while the Bermans would miss their precious little college girl. They'd send someone to the ladies' room or maybe Kate Berman would go herself. How he'd love to see their faces when they finally realized what had happened.

He switched on the light where he remembered Marsha Clark had done so. Carried her down the spiral staircase. At the bottom he set the body down, took the key hanging on the nail to the left, unbolted the door. He picked up the girl again and carried her outside.

He looked all around, then continued on toward the car.

Strapped her into the seat belt and laid her head down against the seat. She might have been sleeping. He pulled away onto the road that led out.

In moments he was on the road heading toward New York City, the night opening endlessly before him.

PART 2

CHAPTER TWENTY-NINE

WHEN he took off the wig Jenny could feel herself—see herself—standing there, watching her—him—taking it off.

Suddenly she sensed for sure he was the killer in the *National Exposé* who murdered Toby and all those others. She opened her mouth to scream but couldn't. She thought she couldn't breathe. Then her breath came in short spasmodic bursts. She needed desperately to grab hold of something, as if something solid could help the way she felt. She shook so badly she felt she'd blow apart. He stamped out. She heard him lock her in.

There was a full bursting feeling in her throat. Her teeth were chattering so she could hear them.

She dug her nails into the palm of her other hand to get control.

It didn't work. Her ears began ringing. Her heart hurled itself unmercifully against her chest.

Stop it! she commanded her body. Every fiber of her was trembling and shaking. Stop!

She tried to take a deep breath but her lungs wouldn't

obey. It was as though she'd fallen beyond the edge of the world. An edge that hadn't been there before.

She pushed her fist into her diaphragm, holding it firmly till her need for air won out. Took four exaggerated breaths.

Dear God, help me!

Another deep breath. Her teeth had all but stopped chattering, but she was still shaking.

Then she heard him at the door. The floor began falling under her.

Please let me live, Jesus.

CHAPTER THIRTY

"**K**ATE Berman?"

"Yes."

"I just don't know how to begin."

"Who is this?"

"Vernon Russel."

"How can I help you, Mr. Russel?"

"It's how I can help you."

"Which is?"

"Which is . . . I've got something I've got to tell some-body."

"I'm listening."

"I'm the one who kidnapped your niece."

Kate let the receiver fall. Rubbed the spot on her breast where she had gotten the sharp, sticking pain. How much longer before the call could be traced?

"Mr. Russel, where are you calling from?"

"I'm in my room in Astoria. But there's other things you should know about me. I did all those killings too."

"I see . . . I'll bet you're also the Gulf Coast Garroter and the Columbus Choker, right?"

"Yes, ma'am. How did you know?"

"Intuition. Do you feel better now?"

"Yes, ma'am."

"Good. Maybe you should consider telling your own doctor about this."

"Is Mrs. Berman there?"

"This is Kate Berman."

"Mrs. Berman?"

"I'm here."

"I have news for you concerning your niece's kidnapping."

She felt she was hanging suspended from the telephone cord.

"I know who's to blame."

"Please . . ."

"You. You married a Christ killer. Then, when the Lord saw fit to take your sister you let a Christ killer be her counterfeit father. He probably—"

Click.

"Kate?"

"Addie?"

"Me. Sorry, Kate . . . Jenny. Heard it on TV."

"Thanks. How are you doing?"

"Like the kids say, hanging in there. Sometimes I can't figure it out, what happened to my life. One day and it was different. I didn't call to talk about that."

"So glad you did call. I miss you."

"Me, too. Anything . . . ?"

"No, not yet. But it'll happen."

"Yeah. I had a kind of breakdown, the doctor says. Or else I would've called before."

"Sorry you had such a hard time. Great to hear from you."

"Josh?"

"Not good. Emmet?"

"Can't believe how nice he's been since . . . Kate?"

"Yes?"

"Get him, Kate. Get him for all of us."

"T-trying."

"I can't talk anymore."

"Can I have the number where you are?"

Addie gave it to her. "Bye."

" 'Care of yourself."

"Hello, Kate."

A deadly confidence told her this was really him.

"People have it backwards."

"What do you mean?" she managed.

"It's revenge that's the best part of living well."

"How do I know you really have her?"

"There's a beauty mark on the top of the small toe of her left foot like a little clod of mud."

She could barely stand.

"Please, how do I know she's alive?"

"Say hello, Jenny."

"Aunt Kate?"

"Thank God."

Click.

Kate stood dazed, feeling as if only the receiver were holding her up.

CHAPTER THIRTY-ONE

KATE and Josh sat across from each other, staring into the gap between them.

When the phone rang Kate ran to it, her pain highlighted by the knowledge that Josh had so little hope that his expression hardly changed.

"I got guys staked in every borough," Casey said at the other end. "I got them waiting in unmarked cars in Brooklyn, Queens, Staten Island. The Bronx. They're in Manhattan dressed as hookers, junkies, bag women and in mufti. On the Island they're housewives wearing hair curlers and mules. Nassau, Suffolk, Westchester, Putnam. Dutchess. Even up to Columbia County. Nothing. How're you doing?"

She felt as though she were constantly peering over the edge of a tall building: legs drained, heart wallowing around as if it'd come loose.

"I'll be all right," she said.

"Josh?"

"Same."

"He'll come around. The tribe don't have them any better than him. Any tribe."

130

"Thanks for calling in, Case."

"I know he's not a drinker but sometimes a couple of snorts can loosen you up."

She thought, He's already too aware of that.

"He was—" she caught the past tense and, feeling compelled to change the karma, said, "He is very devoted to Jenny. Some ways closer than to me."

"We'll get him, Katie."

"Yes, but is it already too late? And even if he doesn't . . . there are things that'll turn a girl crazy . . ."

"Let's not do this. When I think of how we had him at the party—Christ, on a crutch—a freaking chameleon we got here."

"Or the devil." She was glutted with regret and guilt for not having heeded her intuition the night of the party.

"Yeah. Think of something, anything, wake me up."

"You're a good friend, Case."

When she returned Josh had made them each a drink.

After a long while he said, "If life taught me anything, it was how to wait. That's gone, too."

She said nothing, knowing he wasn't inviting her to sell him on the opposite of what he was feeling, knowing he played no games. He needed time.

The swift image of Jenny on her lap, bottle drooping from her mouth, stung her eyes.

"Kill the bastard." She looked at Josh to see if she had spoken or just thought it. He remained numb.

He offered her another drink. She shook her head no and watched him pour an especially large one for himself.

"Easy, Josh."

"You're right. I'm not used to drinking. I might have a hangover in the morning that'll ruin my whole day. Sorry . . ."

"Why don't you go out to the observatory for a while?" she said, trying to keep defeat out of her tone.

131

He nodded, admitting he needed to collect himself before he could help with the search for Jenny.

She watched him put on his coat and lumber out to his sky. To his old coordinates and guideposts. They would all still be there, timeless, even the long dead stars shining down, unperturbed by all the suffering below.

When Josh's parents had both been killed in a car accident after his graduation from med school, he had been disoriented for months. One day, seeing himself in relationship to the stars, he had begun to weep. She knew he would be weeping again before long. The catharsis never failed.

When the door shut she closed her eyes for a moment, trying to escape his pain. Instead she remembered the killer spilling Perrier on Jenny. Why in hell hadn't she listened to herself at the party? Jenny would be safe now. She had let that bastard take her.

CHAPTER THIRTY-TWO

DETECTIVES under Casey's command came and went, avoiding the gloomy and withdrawn Chief's eyes, talking in whispers as though they might somehow avoid his wrath.

Since his wife had died there was no one he felt he could be vulnerable with except Josh and Kate. Tonight that was inappropriate. When his ale buzz had faded to a hum he talked to his twelve-year-old golden lab Molly McGee.

"A nineteen-year-old, sweet as anybody'd want a daughter—what in this fucking world could she do to deserve this?"

Suddenly he remembered meeting Bob Millett at last week's reunion of his old Marine Corps platoon. He started to reach for the phone but remembered Bob had said he'd be on vacation this month.

He rose, trudged to the kitchen for another ale, grateful that Molly McGee still followed him wherever he went in the house. When he was seated again his thoughts returned to the reunion.

"So, Case," Bob had said, "what's with you?"

Casey looked back at the retired state trooper and saw him thirty-five years ago in battle fatigues. He blurted, "Miss the old days, the camaraderie. You're a uniform, you got a partner, the other guys. Too much politics in my job. Chiefs talk to their wives—maybe. I did to mine." He knew he was not one to idealize the past. Neither was Bob. The old days had actually been better for both.

Bob said, "What happened to your old partner McEneaney?"

"Cirrhosis."

"Cop disease."

"That the truth. Such a tough town. I think New Yorkers are jealous that Houston and Detroit and D.C. have higher murder rates. Sometimes I get the feeling New York wants a recount, wants its murderers to work harder."

"Understand."

"You get so nothing's special on the job anymore, you know?"

"I know."

"Find myself at the morgue or a crime scene looking down at something in a body bag used to be somebody, and I find myself thinking that it all keeps going around. Same shit. Just the victims' names change, that's all. Tired of so much blood and misery. Thinking of hanging it up, Bob."

"Cops retire, they eat their gun or drink themselves dead. Miss the job myself, though. This millionaire I told you about, whose estate I run, gives me a house, a car, big bucks, but I can't get used to the idea of being a fucking civilian again."

"Got this one freaking case that's really got me talking to myself."

"One where that animal got your friends' niece?"

"Yeah. Got to solve it before I quit."

Now Casey returned to the kitchen. Poured himself a tall Bushmills. Downed it. Then another. How he missed Moira at times like this. No one had ever been so good at keeping the world away from him.

He looked down at Molly McGee. Gave her a cookie bone.

"Where the fuck is she, girl? *Where?*"

CHAPTER THIRTY-THREE

J ENNY felt like she was on an elevator that was suddenly dropping.

Then she was slapped in the face by a cold wet thing and lost whatever breath she had left. Slowly, she realized it was a towel.

When she looked up his eyes were measuring her in a deeper way than anyone ever had done before. He was gauging her strength and her spirit. She was afraid she might wet herself.

"Here."

The deep timbre of his voice resounded through the soles of her feet and traveled up to her scalp.

She saw that he was holding out a glass of water. Her mouth was a charred hole. She hesitated.

"Take it," he commanded.

She watched her trembling hand reach out. Then she was surprised that she could swallow.

His terrible eyes were mentholated blue. Nothing of him came through them. Except his anger and concentration. Her bowels churned. The way he looked at her . . .

as though she weren't a person. Just a thing. A drop of cold sweat ran down between her breasts.

She waited. Her forearms stung with tiny pricklings and her tongue swelled in her throat. A current of panic shot through her. *God, please don't let me lose control!*

Without warning he reached toward her. She flinched to ward off a blow. Her breathing stopped.

It took another moment before she realized he had reached for the glass.

Control yourself, she thought frantically.

"Make yourself at home," he said and laughed maniacally.

She felt as though her legs were going to give way.

Then he turned his back to her and left, locking her in.

A cold visceral dread seized her that would not be relieved.

CHAPTER THIRTY-FOUR

THE following morning, without deciding, Kate went to an armoire at the second floor landing and took out from under her best linens the Charter Arms .38 special revolver Casey had acquired for her after she'd been stabbed.

It had been a brutal night. She and Josh each kept waking at odd hours. Both had unquenchable thirsts. This morning she kept forgetting things and had to write a list.

" 'Morning."

It was Josh, clean shaven.

"You must've been up early," she said.

"Got fresh squeezed juice. Coffee. Are you hungry?"

She was not, but she was delighted to see a change in his eyes that went beyond his grooming.

After breakfast he said, "Thanks for putting up with me. It's just—"

"I know." She placed a finger over his mouth. He re-lived the loss of his entire family every time she or Jenny was ill or in danger. "All right, let's put my damn good criminologist's head together with the best brains the

New York City M.E.'s office ever had and go to work on this. Going to find our Jenny, Josh."

When he looked up his expression told her he was ready to help. That was all she needed.

"He's expert at disguises," she said. "We know how he went spying at the City Morgue dressed as a redheaded woman. Then he went to Valeur as a writer on architecture. Then to the party. Maybe he's an actor."

"Could be."

"Handsome. Tall. Well built. Very strong. The murders have occurred as often during the day as at night and on weekends, so probably he doesn't work."

"A hair from one of his wigs was real human hair. Expensive. So he's comfortable, maybe rich."

"You're right." Thank God he was with her again.

She continued, "He always chooses women who smoke, so maybe he was abused with cigarettes. Every murder took place in New York State. A biter. Good at electronic surveillance—his parabolic mike. Picked the lock at Valeur. Shaves his head. Uses condoms. Gloves. Cut off a finger probably because he saw blood under the nail. And he gets infuriated if he's insulted. There's a key there somewhere."

"Got to be a way to make that work for us . . ."

"Two main keys," she said. "All the victims being smokers is definitely the commonality, if we can learn what that means to him. And his fury when he's insulted. What?"

"Nothing."

"Nothing is right. What's Casey working on?"

"He's got an army trying to trace him through all three actors' unions. He's even brought in some medium from Boston."

"Next it'll be the Ouija board and then the I Ching."

The rest of the morning went by with Kate reading the

notes and listening to the tapes she had made at the crime scenes. Josh studied the autopsy reports and photographs of the victims.

By afternoon Kate was studying her collection of books on serial killers. Josh made arrangements to have blowups made of the photographs of the victims, planning to paste them up in his study.

At two P.M. Josh made them an omelette. They sat in the dining room. Their meal grew gelid before them.

Kate's thoughts reeled back to her sophomore year of high school. She could still feel her date's powerful pushy hands.

She remembered a frightening moment when she had resisted and found how strong he was. She felt vividly the awful helplessness, the terror, that she was weak and could be forced.

The phone rang.

"He got another one," Casey said.

Kate let the receiver fall.

Come on, where are you?

CHAPTER THIRTY-FIVE

S HE kept thinking, *Don't resist, don't resist.* She was such a coward. She didn't know before how much she wanted to live. She didn't know if it was day or night. She couldn't sleep.

She had no idea where she was. City. Country. There was no air. The silence was absolute. No noise until she made it. Like the outside world had stopped being there. This place was 12 by 12 by 20 (she'd measured it) not including the bathroom. There wasn't even a window. It felt like she was buried.

He had clothes for her here already. Jeans, underwear, blouses. The clothes made her feel like a thing.

She couldn't stand the artificial light. She needed sunlight. Sometimes she even longed for darkness instead of this light.

She heard a jet go by. Very faint. If the people in that plane only knew what they had just flown over.

She was afraid of the future, and she'd go mad living in the present.

She ran to the past.

Uncle Josh stopping his shaving to look at her fascinated

face and give her a surprise shaving-cream kiss. Mailing her postcards when she was sick even if he hadn't been away. The bedtime stories he'd make up in which she was the heroine. The first day of school he wrote WELCOME HOME on a roll of shelf paper and hung it on the front door.

She remembered Aunt Kate asking her what she thought the color of love was. After that she used red for all her gift wrapping.

The treasure hunts with a map and a series of clues that led from one room to the next. The I LOVE YOU message at the end of a surprise book, or an I.O.U. for a trip to the zoo.

Oh God, even these thoughts don't help for long.

She began praying.

A chill seized her. She saw herself in the centerfold of the *Daily News* as the contents of a body bag surrounded by photographs of Aunt Kate and Uncle Josh.

The hair on her neck prickled. She could feel her chest rising and falling no more than an inch in quick breaths. Her entire insides felt as though they had stopped working—still, frozen, solid.

She tried a deep breath but her lungs didn't respond. She shuddered and felt herself begin to tremble.

Then her entire body was shaking. Her teeth chattered.

"Stop it!" she commanded her body. But the shaking and chattering only intensified. Small whimpering noises crawled out of her.

Then she remembered Aunt Kate's words when she'd been too petrified to act in a school play:

"It's okay to be afraid, but panic means you can't function properly anymore. To bring panic back down to fear you have to accept what's happening to you."

She pretended Aunt Kate was right there with her now.

"The shaking is just your body's way of getting out the energy. Don't resist. Exaggerate it."

"I c-can't h-hold . . ."

"Don't. Go with it, Jenny. Feeling won't break you. Holding back will."

"I-I'm a-a-fraid I'll w-wet my s-self."

"Keep shaking, honey. More. Allow the shaking."

Her lunch sprang up back of her throat. She ran to the bathroom on legs that felt as if she were suffering a bout with the flu.

Afterward, holding on to the cold rim of the toilet her entire body wracked with sobs.

After a time she realized she had stopped shaking.

Then she heard him entering.

CHAPTER THIRTY-SIX

IT sickened Kate that she was able to go to her closet, select something from the rack, shower and dress— just as she had always done.

How could she pretend her way through another day when Jenny was the prisoner of a brutal murderer?

In the shower she twisted the hot water knob till it scalded her. She lathered herself violently. As the room steamed she adjusted the cold water knob and punished herself with water that could have been melted ice.

Shortly after midnight it had started to snow in earnest. Now it was piled up in theatrical drifts, laying ermine on the pines. Vapors plumed from the fissures in the Hudson ice, steam rising from countless vats. Schools and businesses had closed early. She had resigned herself to taking the train to Manhattan for her appointment with Casey. Although she preferred driving, she wasn't the navigator Josh was on slippery roads. She had heard on the radio that it was also snowing in Manhattan. That certainly would slow Casey's people. Why had the killer taken Melanie Hines from her apartment into a storm?

Josh entered, speaking to her as if he were continuing a sentence.

" 'Member how much she loves 'the firsts' of each season as she called them? First snow storm, first fire, first oriole, first lawn mowing, first iced tea . . . ?"

"Last night," Kate said, "I dreamt she was a little girl again. I woke remembering her once asking me, 'What's the last number, Aunt Kate?' 'What do you mean?' I said. 'Like z in the alphabet,' she said. I tried to explain how numbers went on forever."

"Like parenting."

"That's for sure."

"Yes . . . But we've got to live, too, while we're trying to find her."

"Right. But Josh . . . I can't stand it much longer."

They held each other tightly.

After a long while Josh said, "Want me to drive you?"

"No, thanks. I'll try to do some writing on the train. It's so hard, but it helps me to feel there's order in the world. Yesterday, when I saw Lilah, I decided I should try at least. Let's not neglect each other now. I need you."

Casey said, "Do you realize how many big handsome male Caucasians between thirty and forty are actors in New York City? Between Actors Equity, Screen Actors Guild and AFTRA we're talking *thousands.*"

"That's why I'm here," Kate said, leaning over his desk. "I don't think he's an actor."

He jumped to his feet.

"Any idea how many people I've had on this?"

"I can imagine. But I've thought some more—I think I steered you wrong. Look, we know psychopaths usually don't make good actors. They're charming and clever and manipulative with language, but they're oblivious to the

145

emotional meaning of words they speak or hear. Ask them what love is and they'll go on and on, but they've never—rarely—felt it themselves. So how can they draw on it to act out?"

"You tell me."

"They can't. That's why their behavior is often inconsistent with what they say and even with their feelings. This is the kind of guy who won't accept his limitations. He boasts and brags that he can act, even creates his own theater. But he simply can't consistently do things in sync with other actors so he's erratic on stage. Acting is reacting."

"You know where this leaves me?"

"Sorry, Case, I had a chance to think it over. I asked myself who would be great at disguises but wouldn't need to be good at words and intentions. Look, it's only an idea. A mime."

"Makes sense. Excuse me." He pressed the intercom. "Lieutenant, I want a briefing nine A.M. sharp tomorrow." He turned to Kate. "What's with the frown?"

Why had the killer risked taking Melanie Hines out of her apartment, passing the doorman again, out into freezing weather? It still gnawed at her.

"Nothing," she said.

CHAPTER THIRTY-SEVEN

HE had only come to bring her dinner. He left immediately.

She wished it was some other time when she was still a student, a niece, instead of a killer's prisoner.

His eyes. They entered hers as if they were lights reaching down into her center.

She was always waiting. Endless terrifying time.

She tried to think of Aunt Kate and Uncle Josh and her friends at school, especially Robbie. But she kept thinking about what would happen if he had a heart attack or something. She couldn't get out. She'd die. She felt she could no longer stand it.

She made her way to the bathroom, opened the spigot marked cold and threw water on her face.

A feeling of aloneness pounced on her so suddenly that she flinched as if to ward off a blow. Became aware of her own quickened blood.

The skin on her scalp and on the pads of her fingertips and the balls of her feet stretched to splitting. Dots appeared behind her eyes. She leaned against the sink for support.

When she looked into the medicine cabinet mirror she saw that her pupils were dilated.

She felt icy. Tremors shook her body.

In desperation she summoned Aunt Kate.

"Shake, Jenny. Go with it. You're a good swimmer. You know you mustn't fight the big waves. Go under them, under your waves of panic. Let them wash over and go past you.

"Remember there's always more than one thing happening to us at once. You can be afraid and brave at the same time. Now push your stomach in with your fist. Harder. Good. Take a deep breath. Another. Stop hunching your shoulders. Pull your tongue away from the roof of your mouth. Breathe. Let your shoulders go loose."

"T-the shaking . . . it's stopping itself."

A twinge at the back of her neck had swelled into a headache. But the shaking, the panic, had subsided.

"Keep breathing deeply sweetheart. Even if the flash of panic feels like it'll singe your hair, remember it can't kill you. Can't even hurt you. Float and let time pass and you'll be free of it. When the fear is becoming panic try to get yourself involved in something."

Exercise, Jenny thought. Read. Write!

He was at the door!

Bad as it is, please let me live, Jesus.

CHAPTER THIRTY-EIGHT

"IT's Case, Kate."

"What've you got?" Her nerves were being stretched more and more tightly like strings on guitar pegs.

"Zero. Every mime in the city. Upstate. Jersey. Connecticut. All the schools for mimes. I even had the clowns checked out. Nothing. Any ideas?"

"I was going to call you. Still can't get it out of my head that he took Melanie Hines out of the apartment to kill her in a snowstorm. Why? I want to try something different."

"I'm open for the world being proved flat."

"I'd like you to find me an actor with the same build as our killer. Have him dressed in a ski parka. It would be good if the same doorman could be on duty, too, and both be filled in on what we're doing."

"You want to get into Melanie Hines' head."

"Case, you missed your vocation."

"I know, should've been a detective. You realize I'll have to get permission from the new tenants."

"And one more thing."

"What?"

"I want to do it today."

"While it's snowing. Figures."

A ring from the lobby intercom. Kate picked up the receiver, feeling Melanie's fear.

"There's a Frank O'Rourke here, Miss Hines."

Thank God!

"Send him up, Charlie."

Finally. All over now. Then why am I shaking?

The sound of the doorbell made her jump.

"Y-yes?"

"Frank O'Rourke, Melanie."

She looked through the peephole. He was dressed in a parka, just like Nora said he would be.

The chains and bolts would not cooperate with her hands. Finally, she got the door open.

His size comforted her a little.

"Am I glad to see you!" She looked down the hall both ways. "C'mon in. I'll just get my coat. You don't mind, I just want to get out of here."

"I don't mind."

She took her coat from the closet and threw a scarf round her neck.

"Sorry I'm acting so funny. Scared me to death."

"I understand. You're safe now."

So why was she so cold in spite of her coat and scarf in a heated apartment?

"Thanks. And thanks for coming out in this storm."

"Any friend of Nora's."

She made her mouth smile as she locked the door.

In the elevator she stood close to him. Maybe that maniac was outside waiting for them.

She was startled by the elevator stopping. *Easy, now.*

As they walked out of the building she looked into the doorman's eyes.

" 'Night, Charlie."

" 'Night, Miss Hines."

" 'Night," she heard Frank O'Rourke say in a friendly way. She was struck by the tone. But didn't know why. He was smiling too, though he hadn't smiled since she'd met him. Not really smiled. Probably just her imagination from being scared.

Outside, the cold and wet made her shiver.

He took her arm.

"E-excuse me," she said after he began pulling her along toward a car at the curb. "I thought you walked over."

"I did. But now we're going to get out of the snow a while so we can talk like we did over the phone."

It was as if the wind had suddenly stopped just in the space around her. Now she knew why she had thought it unusual that he had smiled at the doorman on the way out like he was—what was the word—*proud,* that's it! More than just enjoying himself . . .

"Get in the back seat! And if I hear one scream—"

"It's okay, Kevin. You can stop now."

"Find out what you needed to know?"

"Hope so."

"Let me get this straight, Kate," Casey said as he paced his office. "First you have me call off our search for an actor with the largest task force since D-Day. Then I look for a mime. And now you're convinced he *is* an actor."

"No. I still don't think he's an actor. But I do know he got a huge kick from getting past the doorman with Melanie. It was . . . a kind of performance for him. Know what I mean?"

"No."

"Makes two of us."

"Maybe you need to lay off for a while, Katie. This case—"

"Don't you start treating me like a girl, Bill Casey. I'll lay off when Jenny's home."

"Sorry."

"Look, I'm confused, I admit it. I just came here to tell you what I'm feeling."

"Want me to drop the mimes and start the routine again with the actors?"

"No."

"What do you want?"

"To go home and think."

CHAPTER THIRTY-NINE

"WHAT does 'method to your madness' mean, Kate?" said Lilah.

Kate leaned back in her chair. "It means if someone does something hard to understand, instead of calling it crazy or madness you try to assume that there is a purpose, a method, a good reason why they've done it. Then you'll have a better chance of figuring out why they've done it." It hurt to look at Lilah's young innocent face. Jenny . . . She had to be here, though. She needed the order and rewards of her work. And Lilah and the others needed her.

"I don't understand." Lilah said.

"Okay. Let's say that a person doesn't know anything about autism. We bring them here to the institute to visit. They see kids behaving differently from most other kids. To most of you here at the institute routine is very important, touching can be painful. Our guest might come away thinking people with autism are crazy. But if our guest thinks there must be a good reason why you are all so different—in other words, finds a 'method to the madness'—our guest will then be open to learning the truth.

When we figure out the method we know it isn't madness. Understand, honey?"

"I understand, and I also want you to explain it with more 'in other words.'"

"Good!"

It amazed Kate that Lilah, for whom communication was so difficult, knew enough to use "and" when appropriate instead of "but." Few people did.

"That's enough for today, honey, I think. You're doing great."

"I . . ."

"Yes, what is it, sweetheart?"

"I don't know how to say it."

"Try. I'll help you."

"I love Jenny. Sorry someone took her. I love you."

Kate's cheeks were wet. Despite all her problems with communication, the girl had managed to convey three separate distinct messages in three simple sentences.

"I love you too, Lilah. Thanks. And I know Jenny knows you love her."

Later that day, Kate had begun writing in her book but set her pen down. Maybe she could use the "method to madness" reasoning to help her with the haunting question of why the killer had taken Melanie outdoors in a snowstorm to kill her.

She thought about what she'd learned from the walkthrough to get inside Melanie's head. She thought about mimes.

But she was still puzzled. It took forever for her to reach a hand up and wipe her brow.

She picked up her pen and wrote.

Instead of saying it's a contradiction that a psychopath (who would be a poor actor) is proud of the "performance" he gives while taking Melanie past the doorman of her

*building, I must assume that this contradiction makes
sense.*

*Under what circumstances might this psychopath, i.e.,
poor actor, be so proud of his performance?*

She stared at the sentences, thinking. Finally, she saw
what she had been missing. She leaped to her feet. Went
to the den. Punched in Casey's number.

"Case? Me. Sure he's a bad actor, but there're a lot of
bad actors out there who like to act. Maybe he tried acting
and wasn't good at it."

"What am I supposed to be looking for now—an amateur?"

"Yes. Maybe a student."

"Jesus, Mary and Joseph. There's got to be even more
acting students than actors."

"You're right."

"Sorry, Kate. Great work. I'll get on it right now."

Right now, still didn't change the fact that tomorrow
would be the first Christmas without Jenny.

Tonight, she knew, she'd wait, even in her sleep.

CHAPTER FORTY

THE additional detectives recently acquired at the request of Chief Casey had begun jamming the briefing room.

The Chief stood looking out a window. Torrential rain puddled the sidewalks, made the gutters run with filth. The day matched his mood exactly.

When he turned and looked around at the faces he saw the fatigue, the damaged professional pride, because they hadn't come up with anything solid. He braced himself for what he had to say.

"I know who the killer is."

The room broke into tumult.

Casey raised his hands.

"So do you. We know it's a male Caucasian. We know how tall he is. How he's built. His strength. We know he's probably rich. We know his sickness is going to need to be fed more and more, faster and faster. All we need is his name."

He looked over the faces. He had not only succeeded in getting their full attention, there was hope now in some eyes.

"According to the file and your reports every acting and mime school in all the boroughs came up empty. Okay. Mackin, Perkowski, pick a team and check out every acting school ever went out of business. Phone company throws out old yellow page books. Forty-Second Street library. Third floor. Microfilm desk. Everything you need. Where's Mackin?"

"Here Chief."

"After we got a list you and Perkowski pick a team of partners for Manhattan. The biggest team'll be Manhattan 'cause that's where most of the schools are."

"Right Chief."

"Kopec, you choose a team for Queens. Bottinni, Bronx. Sugarman, Brooklyn. Kelsey, Staten Island. You're thinking you need say ten or twelve people for your team, take twelve. People we got. We need to get this bastard. *Now.* Yeah Bottinni?"

"How far you want us to go back in the phone books?"

"Routine, Bottinni, remember? We don't know how old our man is. Go back enough to make sure you cover all possibilities. Meggett?"

"Now we got the lists and we go back to the schools we already hit and ask if they knew teachers at these schools."

"So?" Casey said.

"So, a lot of these teachers'll be dead. They won't remember. They'll be living somewhere else."

A few scattered groans.

Casey brought his fist down on the table. "That attitude is exactly why we don't have this freaking hairball yet! They're living somewhere else, there's phones, Meggett. There's cars, airplanes if you need them. They don't remember, you ask the kind of questions makes them remember. They're dead, you got other teachers taught at the same school. Didn't you people ever read a goddamn police procedure book? Anybody ever watches television knows you catch animals like this with routine. Not witnesses. Not raids. Not lineups. Not decoys. Legwork. Interviews. Details. R-O-U-T-I-N-E. Good-night-Irene."

The packed room was soundless.

"This is a running assignment. Twenty-four hours a day. Every day till we score. All my fighting to get more people. We got more people now they got beggars in India. So use them. Use them like this guy is going to do your mother or your sister next. We need urgency here. Urgency and—*what* Meggett?"

"R-routine, sir."

"All right. These serial guys don't believe they'll ever get caught. Invincible, the shrinks say. You may not believe this but it's a matter of who wants more. Does this scumball want to kill more than we want to capture him. Do we want to catch him more than he wants to kill.

"That's enough for now. I had Sy's deli fix up some platters. Corned beef, pastrami, knishes."

"Way to go Chief," someone called.

"Yeah, a long way," Casey said. "Lunch and we hit the streets."

Conversations started up.

"One more thing," Casey said.

The room quieted.

"Any man, any woman, any team that comes up with this animal's name gets a week in Atlantic City with my Gold Card."

Cheers and whistles.

"Can we bring our wives or husbands?" a female voice familiar to Casey called from the rear.

"Kelsey, you are one horny detective."

CHAPTER FORTY-ONE

J ENNY felt overwhelmed by his unyielding evil. If she could get him talking, to trust her a bit, could she find a way to escape?

She watched him set down the tray of food. His eyes could be so beautiful. Beetle-wing-blue now in this light.

She had to draw so deeply for her voice it emerged as a call: "P-please don't go."

Far away at the extreme rim of Nasson's concentration something stirred, a subtle hint of light. Something terrifying yet needed approached him.

The way he stood watching her like an animal in a zoo made her sorry for having asked. *Don't panic.*

"D-do you think I could have a pencil and some paper, please?"

She threw her hair back in such a natural, unaffected way it pleased him.

Why not talk to her—she's mine, isn't she?

He said, "What's the paper and pencil for?"

Calm. Be calm. "I want to be a writer. Do you like to read?"

"Yes."

The mixture of fear and exhaustion had suddenly made her sleepy—of all things!

She yawned. She made doing such an ugly thing delicate.

"What?" she said.

"What do you mean 'what'?"

"What do you like to read?"

"Only the truth, to learn."

"But fiction *is* the truth."

"I have no time for stories."

He said this with such force she decided not to continue. The bubble of fear threatened to burst into panic. She imagined a wave washing over her.

"Do you think I could have a book?"

"Which one?"

Had she really been asked to make such an impossible choice?

"Winesburg, Ohio by Sherwood Anderson."

"Stories?"

"Magical ones, about a boy who wants to be a newspaperman, and the people in the town he lives in."

"Okay."

"Don't go, please." She had never met anyone so indifferent. So by himself. Clinical.

"What else, *Robinson Crusoe*?"

He laughed without the faintest hint of good-naturedness, or of sarcasm. Chilling. In a way younger than she. Undeveloped. She must get away. He was too strong for anything but cunning. But how? Maybe if she kept talking to him, learning . . .

He was amazed that she did not try to strike him back with words. She did not change hurt to anger. Instead she showed her hurt. Could she possibly have what was extinct in her sex—innocence?

"I'll bring you *Robinson Crusoe* , too."

"Thank you. This is very much like being shipwrecked, you know."

Fear wrapped around her but she felt her mouth form a sweet, agreeable expression.

Nasson saw her form that special look that women put on for men. He got to his feet, furious that he had thought her innocent.

When he wheeled to leave she said, "Please, let's talk again, soon."

The way he looked at her! Like he was calculating just how hard a blow would kill her. For a blazing instant she thought she was going to lose control.

When he left she was grateful. And angry with herself for being so transparently friendly, so false. How had he been able to spot it so exactly?

She remembered something she'd read in one of Aunt Kate's books about psychopaths:

"The deranged and the persistently hunted acquire a sort of intuition others don't have."

She lay in terror at the prospect of outwitting him.

CHAPTER FORTY-TWO

DETECTIVE Wally Mackin said to his partner behind the wheel, "The case of the actor in the haystack."

Mackin was slight with eyes like curdled milk. He had a fierce expression his partner guessed he had developed because he had had scarring acne as a boy.

"Twenty-nine fucking acting schools," Mackin went on, "then mimes and now actors again. I could turn producer."

"I could never be so lucky," Frank Perkowski said and then roared, throwing back his huge head. His jowled and wattled face shook as he laughed.

Mackin said, "One of your Polish friends gets collared for rape. They bring him in for a lineup. The broad walks in, he goes, 'That's her! That's her!' "

"Fuck're you doing? I said enough with the Polish jokes."

"You're right. A guy in a garbage truck goes through a Polish neighborhood—"

"Fucking harp."

"—yelling, 'Garbage! Garbage!' Polish lady opens her

window, yells down, 'I'll take three bags.' Here we are, nineteen Gramercy."

"Who did you say gave you my name?"

Mackin leaned close to the old woman and looked at her cosmetic-free face, her eyes of green quartz, the barely jutting chin, the shiny gray hair, full mouth and the slightly equine nose that alone kept her from being beautiful. He thought how her strong face was at odds with her shrunken body. Somehow a brave contradiction.

"I said it was Jules Farcus, Mrs. Jennings."

"Jules, of course. Lovely man. We taught at Frank Robert's studio for a time. You said his name on the phone, didn't you?"

"That's right, ma'am," Perkowski said. "Now," he pulled out the artist's rendering, "we'd like you please to look at this sketch and see if you can remember the face. 'Course you have to imagine the face much younger."

She took the sketch with her twig-like fingers. "How much younger?"

Mackin said, "From when you taught at T. J. Studios."

"I thought you wanted to know about my time at Frank Robert's?"

"No, ma'am," Perkowski said. "T. J. Studio. How long ago was that?"

"My hair was blonde then. Natural, I mean."

"I'm sure," Perkowski said. "How long ago?"

"I have pictures. Over there in the credenza. That's me sitting on the davenport."

Perkowski, hoping the frustration in Mackin's face wouldn't get into his voice, went and got the framed photograph. "You were beautiful, ma'am. But, forgive me, this picture was taken when you were what—twenty?"

"Nineteen."

"Nineteen," Mackin repeated and rubbed the back of his neck.

Perkowski said, "We're talking about the years you were at T. J. Studio, ma'am. Please look at the sketch. Imagine the man much younger. T. J. Studio went out of business eighteen years ago."

"I thought you wanted to see my hair blond."

Mackin muttered an obscenity. Perkowski was relieved to see the old woman hadn't heard.

Perkowski said, "This is very important, ma'am. This man is the serial killer you've been seeing in the papers, TV. We need your help desperately. Take all the time you need. Imagine the face younger. Maybe even with a mustache or beard at the time. That's it. What? You recognize him? Tell me, Mrs. Jennings. Please."

"Who did you say gave you my name?"

CHAPTER FORTY-THREE

I *must be crazy. I'm keeping a journal. But, no—I'm writing to keep from going crazy. Aunt Kate was right. It helps to do something.*

Strange, when I write it's like there're three, four of me trying to talk.

The worst is the fear—but I'm writing to try to stop thinking about that. The endless time I have to get through is brutal.

This morning I could have sworn I heard children's voices outside the rear wall. The way they shriek when they're playing. Just as quickly they were gone. Then a dog barking off in a distance. Made things worse thinking they were so close. If I can trust my ears anymore.

I lose my bearings.

Anyone who's been in prison would understand. You become different to yourself in a weird way. I looked into the bathroom mirror and thought, could this be me—this gray-faced witch with blood in her eyes and broom-straw hair?

I look at my face trying to figure out what I'm thinking from my eyes. Then it becomes unreal. It becomes someone else's face. I have to struggle to get back to reality, whatever that is.

Keep thinking about "Anne Frank." "The Man in the Iron Mask." All the movies with dungeons and prisons. All over the world millions of people in prisons. I feel a little comforted by their company.

This place gets tinier and tinier. I feel it shrinking. Makes me want to scream. I don't have the words to write it. Like a constant, low-grade panic. Yesterday I felt I could no longer stand it.

Then, slowly, I began to look at the room differently. And I started to see things I hadn't noticed before. The bed, the chair, the place where the walls met the ceiling had various shadows in the lamplight.

I began to concentrate even more. The same room that had just felt so oppressively the same was different. Even beautiful. My experience of it had changed, my eyes refreshed. I looked at the shadows for a long time. Probably I fell asleep, but I'm not sure.

This is the worst possible time to die. We'll be on Mars soon, Uncle Josh says. I love my era. I want to marry a man like Robbie. Kids. I need to experience so much.

I spend all day sometimes thinking about my plan to get out of here.

After he brought my cold chicken today I asked him please to stay. I needed to talk to someone. Even him.

"You only think you know what being alone is," he said.

"What about all these weeks I've been here?"

"People miss you."

At that moment he actually looked younger than me in a way I can't quite say. Older, but with younger eyes. Eyes like light blue silk.

"Don't you have anyone?" I said.

The silk darkened. I never saw anybody look that hard.

"DON'T YOU EVER PITY ME!" he yelled.

I felt as if my ears were being pushed together.

Then he left.

I felt myself physically shrinking.

Endless.

166

CHAPTER FORTY-FOUR

N ASSON used the washer and dryer in the basement to do their laundry. Never know what could get back to the wrong party from a dry cleaner. Today when he came in she was reading another book. He liked the way she read the books he brought her. The delicate way in which she turned the pages. She had washed her hair.

"Please, would you let me see a little daylight?"

"Absolutely not."

Her eyes didn't seem frightened. She looked brave, as though she was determined not to be afraid. Not like the others.

"You could tie me up and gag me. Please. I need to smell the outside."

She made him feel like a cruel master. But then he caught himself. Life was no more than a constant series of small betrayals, lies. He had never seen shinier, more beautiful hair. He yearned to touch, stroke it.

She began to cry.

Though he didn't understand, it upset him when she cried.

"Please! It's just that there's so much time to get through. I won't try anything. I swear."

The way she spoke, he knew she meant it. Sometimes he felt she wasn't lying, which frightened him. Her sweet beauty confused him at times. He didn't know quite what to feel. What he should do.

"I feel I'm always waiting," she pleaded.

It wasn't so much what she was saying. He liked listening, talking. He had forgotten. But a part of him couldn't bear to see her so unhappy.

"We'll see," he said.

He liked the light that went on in her eyes . . . Her innocent face . . .

"Oh thank you! I mean thanks for considering it. That would be so great!"

Maybe she was beginning to see him for the kind master he was. He wanted her to throw back her hair in that simple, unaffected way he liked so much.

"Thanks again."

There was something so considerate about her he felt compelled to be considerate also. She kind of expected it without being disrespectful. He could see she was used to a world where people just were considerate. Still, he didn't know whether to trust her. Or, if he should.

He knew if she stood her head would only come up to his shoulder. He wanted to stay and look at her hair and feel her niceness. Yet, he felt she couldn't be trusted.

She smiled at him. He had never seen her so full of hope.

What she felt he felt.

"Where are you going?" she said.

He didn't answer, not wanting her to hear the feelings that his voice might give away.

* * *

That evening he went out for the newspapers to read about himself. On the front page of the *News* was the headline: **DISTRAUGHT!** Underneath was a photograph of Kate and Josh Berman's faces twisted with anguish. Triumph straightened his shoulders and put a lightness in his stride.

He turned from the kiosk on Sixth Avenue and there was *the* smell. Like walking into a wall. It was an odor no amount of time or distance could erase from his memory. Hate and desire mushroomed in him. He spun round to see the woman who was emitting the scent step into a Checker. He was glad a tiny piece of her black mink had gotten caught in the door.

Nasson imagined the smell was still inside him, staining his skin and clothing. Once he had tried to discover through a perfumer exactly what it consisted of. Musk certainly, he had learned. And jasmine, no doubt. Maybe essence of orange bloom and bergamot, perhaps. But Nasson had abandoned the idea. He had long known the source of his pain. To be able to smell it more distinctly would not soften its blow.

Now he imagined the odor. At once it stank and intoxicated. Bliss and torture. He knew he must hurry home before he felt the rest.

Slamming the door behind him, he bolted the lock. Pressed his back against the wall of the entrance hall in the dark hoping for his breath to return.

Slid down till he sat on the floor. Hard as he fought, the mixture of fetidness and fragrance made him see Her beauty. She was smooth as dark honey. Sweet and salty and sticky. Holding Her round arms out with a syrupy gesture in a cloud of blue smoke. Then Her deep voice:

Embrace me, my sweet embraceable you
Embrace me, you irreplaceable you.

169

As Nasson sat in the dark his head, torso, hands and feet shrank to childlike proportion. He was small and alone and it was familiar.

From outside himself he could hear whimperings. He didn't know he was crying. He felt a rush of wetness running down his thighs.

CHAPTER FORTY-FIVE

AFTER showering, Jenny put her clothes on slowly and carefully buttoned them with an old childhood feeling of accomplishment that came to her often now, when life was especially crushing. In an effort to stop the terrible thoughts that came on her like another kind of rain she began to write.

Yesterday I lay in the dark for hours thinking how impossible the loss of freedom and privacy is to write about. All I could come up with was "It takes the life out of life," which certainly didn't begin to say it.

Suddenly I didn't want to write any more. Only to experience. I'm tired of knowing things from books but not from living. If only I could get out I'd be so grateful.

I miss Robbie but lately he seems a little young to me. He's beautiful but so vain. Some boys protest the system with one hand and clip their trust fund bonds with the other. Robbie doesn't even protest. His kids would be so beautiful . . . outside, anyway. They'd have to get soul from someone else.

Last night I dreamed about someone I might meet someday. A man touching me at the back of my neck. We were

171

*at a party and he looked different from the others. Just a
little taller than me. Adult eyes but not jaded. Amused.
Younger than Robbie's somehow. A slight scent of shaving
lotion like newly mown grass. We talked about good
books. He liked me. Thought I was interesting. I woke even
more desperate to escape.*

*After he brings me my meals he stays sometimes. We
read together in the same room. Very weird. There's no
way I want us to be together. But we are together. Our
destinies are joined. Once I even felt the weight of the
sadness of his life. Uncanny.*

*Now I'm thinking I don't want to be a clever writer. And
I certainly don't need to be famous.*

*Maybe I'll just write about things I love, like how dogs
lie in the sun like turned-over roller skates.*

*Or will I just be considered hokey? I don't know. If
there's one thing I learned here it's that there's so much I
don't know. I do know I'll learn faster if I ever get out,
though, because I'm more willing to change. Writing isn't
helping with the fear much now. My body feels so hot my
tears seem like little drops of melted wax—*

Wait—he's here now.

*The first thing I asked him was whether he was going to
let me go outside—bound and gagged, of course.*

He told me it was snowing.

I could hardly contain myself—he didn't say no.

I told him I love the snow. I do.

He looked at me a long time, studying me.

He said okay, since it was Christmas.

*I wasn't going to let not being home for Christmas spoil
going outside. I wasn't, but I couldn't help it.*

*He tied my hands and feet with cord and put a handker-
chief in my mouth. Then he carried me out of my room.*

Seeing where he lived I felt like a kid allowed to do a

grownup thing. Drink coffee. Stay up late. I didn't remember ever being so happy.

He carried me wrapped in a blanket and scarf out into the hallway. There was a great big bannister. It was a house, not an apartment.

He took me up a flight of stairs, set me down, and opened a door.

Snow was kissing my face. I was breathing fresh air full of living smells. I heard the wonderful honk of horns. And people. I cried. My legs felt as though they contained springs that had been held back under terrific pressure and just now had been released. If I couldn't run soon I'd lift off and fly.

I could tell it was the city. I was torn between simply enjoying my time, or making the most of it to plan my escape. He had placed me behind the slightly opened door so I couldn't be seen from any of the neighboring houses and apartments. The blanket hid my bindings and the scarf covered my gag.

I was shocked that people were going about their business. Didn't they know how dangerous a place the world is?

"Someone rang the front bell," he whispered. "We're going down."

I hadn't heard anything. For an instant I was crushed to be leaving so soon.

Then I realized the significance of what he had said.

CHAPTER FORTY-SIX

As he pulled her inside and closed the door behind them, her heart beat like stomping feet.

He set her down, bound and gagged, in the nearest room. Closed the door and hurried out.

She looked around—there was a window!

What she heard next made her feel as if she was already partially free.

". . . neighbor . . . lost . . . cat . . ."

If she could hear this well from here why was everything nearly soundless from her room? He definitely must have it soundproofed.

She stuck her tongue out trying to free the handkerchief. It wouldn't budge.

Began banging her head against the floor, but the carpet absorbed most of the sound.

If she could make her way over to the window, then manage to get on her feet, she could smash the glass with her elbow and whoever was downstairs would hear her.

". . . renting . . . they're away . . ."

She heard Nasson's voice louder now—they were coming up the stairs!

Jenny reversed her direction. If she could get to the door in time and manage to kick it . . . *Hurry . . . hurry . . . hurry . . .* She inched her way across the floor. Thought to roll herself which went quicker.

Meow.

The cat—they're right outside the door now!

"*Here's* my Timothy. C'mon boy."

Please wait, please.

She could hear the sound of two sets of feet padding down the stairs.

With all her strength Jenny rolled herself faster. Sweat dripped into her eyes. Finally she butted against the door.

". . . bye . . . thanks."

Here I am!

The bitter sound of the front door slamming made her heart descend.

With a reserve of energy she didn't know she possessed she began tumbling toward the window. When she at last reached it she heard him opening the door of the room.

A balloon in her emptied. She tried a deep breath but could only manage a shallow one. There was a needle-sharp pain behind and below her optic nerve. Her whole face sank. Then the rest of her. Sadness and frustrations poured out of her heart and she fought the tears. She had better not make herself look suspicious or she'd never have another chance to escape.

He picked her up and carried her out to the windowless room. Removed the handkerchief and binds.

When she called on her voice, it had to travel up from the deepest part of her.

"Please, can't I get some air now that he's gone?"

"Tomorrow. Maybe."

The balloon in her filled.

Tomorrow she would be ready with a plan.

175

CHAPTER FORTY-SEVEN

"You know why Polacks can't make ice cubes?"

"Goddamn you Mackin. I'm going to make a change-of-partner request to Casey."

"Sure you will." He stopped for a red light. "They can't make ice cubes 'cause they lost the recipe."

Perkowski's huge head was turned toward his window. He saw nothing as he tried to sort his anger at his partner from his exhaustion and frustration that the entire task force had still not come up with a solid clue. Finally, he said, "Know how to save a drowning Irishman? Just answer yes or no."

"No."

"Good."

Mackin burst out laughing. The car swerved.

Perkowski said, "Happy now you brought me down to your level?"

Mackin tried to answer but he was laughing too hard. Finally he said, "You're very funny, you know that?"

Perkowski turned and looked at Mackin's fierce features grinning. He had rarely seen his partner look so happy. "Really think so?"

176

"Sure. Got any more?"

Perkowski was surprised to feel a smile move his lips. He sat up in his seat, trying to remember how the one went about the definition of an Irish physicist.

At the entrance to Duane Travers' Greenwich Village apartment a housekeeper asked them to wait.

"A prime candidate for breast reduction, wouldn't you say?" Mackin said.

Perkowski frowned and shook his head.

When the housekeeper returned she led them to a large room where a window looked out on the Morton Street pier. Perkowski thanked her.

Mackin pointed to the long wooden finger of a pier jutting out into the waters of the Hudson. "Also known as Fire Island West."

"Lay off the gays, Mack. They have to live, too."

"Never mind. Let's do what we came here for."

There were bookshelves containing dozens of pamphlet-like copies of plays published by Samuel French, framed covers of old *Playbills*, advertisements for plays, reviews, collected works of Shakespeare and Chekov, various anthologies of plays.

"I'm sorry to keep you waiting."

They looked up.

Travers' chestnut hair covered his ears and was as lush as a symphony conductor's. Through the short, wire mesh hair in the middle of the scalp they could see the unmistakable pink, round knittings of hair transplants. He was in his sixties. His skin was translucent, his slight body tight. He was wearing black chinos and a powder blue boatneck sweater. Gray hair sprang through the cuffs.

"How can I help you?" Travers said mellifluously.

"We have a police artist's sketch here," Mackin said, "of

a suspected perpetrator. We'd like you to see if he was ever a student of yours at Horizon Studio before they went out of business."

"Do you have any idea how many students I had there over the years?"

"Unfortunately, we do," Perkowski said. "This sketch is of a murderer."

"Let me see," Travers said, extending a hand.

He studied the sketch, then took a pair of granny glasses from his desk and studied some more.

After a while he said, "How tall do you think he is?"

"Six feet," Perkowski said.

Travers said, "It could be . . . what else can you tell me about him?"

Mackin said, "Very strong. Between thirty and forty. Smart. Rich. Real good at disguises."

"Certainly sounds like Carl," Travers said.

Perkowski and Mackin looked at each other, controlling their excitement.

"Carl who?" Mackin said, taking out a notepad and pen.

"Nasson."

"Spell it."

Travers did. "You say he could be a *murderer*?"

Mackin said, "We think he could be the serial murderer."

"You're joking." Travers pulled off his glasses.

"Look at me, Mr. Travers."

"You're not joking. Jesus. What's next?"

"Next, I'm going to call my chief."

CHAPTER FORTY-EIGHT

J ENNY didn't miss having her period. She was glad she didn't have to ask him for tampons. And she wasn't worried—she was careful about her pills because of Robbie.

But she did wonder if she would ever have one again. She had read that women in concentration camps stopped menstruating because of the stress and the absence of night, day and clocks.

Also, although she didn't know for how long exactly, her sleep-wake cycle had changed radically. She tended to be up what she estimated was twenty to twenty-five hours at a time. Then slept about ten hours.

Despite all her baths and showers, her loss of privacy prevented her from feeling clean.

Knowing other people were so close by yet were aware of nothing made things even worse.

When she escaped she would have to reevaluate her relationship with Robbie. She realized now they had different sorts of hearts.

Jenny knew she wouldn't be allowed outside before nightfall when there'd be less chance of being seen.

She picked up her only pencil, considered breaking it at the right place now to begin testing her plan. But she might want to write before dinner. Also, he might spot it broken and suspect something. She would ask to go outside when he brought her dinner. When he left, she would eat a bit then break the pencil and practice for a while before he came to pick up her tray.

Time slowed. Stopped. Went backward.

When he brought lunch, she had smiled and thanked him. She had complimented him on his shirt, careful not to overdo it. She didn't show her fear, but it was there all right. She could live with the fear. It was the panic that was intolerable.

"Please, can I get some fresh air later?"

He surprised her by hesitating. She had assumed his "We'll see" yesterday was a good sign of probability if not certainty. It was as if she had fallen from a great height. Was still falling.

"Maybe," he finally said.

The breath escaped suddenly from her lungs as though she had been punched on her back.

When he had gone she thought, He's playing with me, and fought against a rush of hysteria.

After a time she was able to cry which always helped her cope.

Despite not being hungry she forced herself to eat a little of the ham and cheese sandwich to give her strength for later. What remained she flushed down the toilet so he wouldn't see anything out of the ordinary.

She tried reading but couldn't concentrate. Same for writing.

Measured the pencil with her eye then snapped it in two. She placed the smaller piece of pencil in her mouth holding it with her teeth.

It was still too long so that he might notice. Now, what?

She looked around her cell. Nothing. Holding one end of the broken pencil in her fingers she began chewing off the other end.

The taste evoked memories of pencils she had chewed as a little girl. Crayons. Building blocks. Milk through straws. Cookies. When she saw the image of Aunt Kate waiting for her with galoshes because it had been sunny when she left for school that long ago morning, hot tears poured from her eyes.

She fought the tears, not wanting her eyes to look swollen for him. Not wanting anything but the usual, so he might, please God, say yes.

When she placed the entire pencil back in her mouth it fit perfectly. She stuffed a handkerchief in her mouth. Began working at it with the pencil.

Damn, this was harder than she had imagined.

When, finally, the handkerchief fell from her mouth, her heart ascended in her chest.

Jenny practiced till her mouth ached. Rested. Practiced some more, this time in the bathroom in case he came in and found her with a handkerchief stuffed in her mouth.

She was afraid to practice any more because of a possible cramp in her face muscles. She stopped and lay unable to do anything more than wait.

He brought dinner. She searched his features for a clue to his mood. But his face gave nothing away.

She barely ate the cold hamburger and the french fries which tasted like shirtboard. Disposed of the remains in the usual way.

When, finally, he came for her tray, she blurted, "Please, can I go outside with you for just a little while?"

"It's raining."

"I don't mind a little nice rain."

"For a while."

She was delighted, yet angry. All those hours of fearing

181

he would say no. And now he seemed to have completely forgotten his earlier doubts. Or was he just torturing her with this abrupt change?

"Thank you."

He left with her tray.

When he returned, dressed in a parka, with her bindings and gag, scarf and blanket, she already had the pencil in her mouth.

What if he asked her a question? She couldn't answer without the pencil giving her away.

"Sure you don't want to do this another time?"

She shook her head and implored him with her eyes.

He bound and gagged her and wrapped the scarf and blanket around like the last time.

"Less people out in the rain," he said.

She would not allow herself to be disappointed. Couldn't have waited any longer anyway.

As he carried her out of her room, excitement made her chest rise and fall rapidly.

Being carried up the steps to the roof, she concentrated on normalizing her breathing so as not to alert him.

When she felt herself being set down she blinked her eyes open. He was opening the door to the roof.

A cold damp gust chilled, making her feel even more vulnerable. Yet even the natural dark of night was comforting.

He carried her outside and they both crowded behind the door.

She looked up at Uncle Josh's sky. *Please, Mother of God, help me do this.*

She began working the pencil against the gag.

Almost at once the rain fell harder. Her pulse pounded between her eyes.

The drops grew larger as the downpour intensified. If

she didn't succeed soon, who would hear her in such a rain?

Her stomach and bowels were queasy.

Water pounded down in a curtain of nearly solid gray.

"This is crazy!" he shouted over the gale.

The handkerchief fell from her mouth.

"Help!"

She felt her face come up to hit his hand. Tasted blood on her gums. Happened so quickly, the surprise of the blow and the pain melded together. She had to yell again. Someone had to hear.

"H—"

He struck her again.

She felt her eyes roll back.

CHAPTER FORTY-NINE

OUTSIDE the Waldorf Towers the sun was shining, but Kate noted that Carl Nasson's room would be dark without the artificial light. All around her, forensic people were on their knees, working with tweezers and plastic envelopes and dusting for prints. She ached with disappointment.

By how much time had they missed him?

Casey said, "No prints, of course."

She nodded absently, thinking that she had never been in a more sterile living space. The absence of color and warmth were chilling.

There was not a single houseplant—either stationary pot or hanging. Nor a trace of a dog, cat, bird or fish. No hint of a favorite chair or nook or corner. Not one work of fiction among all the many books. Not one bag of junk food. Nothing cozy, frivolous or sentimental. Nothing *human*.

"So," Casey said as men moved behind him, clipboards in their hands, scattering stacks of oak tag tickets on the floor, "we know this joint won't ever make the monthly spread in *Better Homes and Gardens*. What else?"

"More than that, Case. It's not civilized. Not one inkling anyone lived here."

A detective handed Casey a manila envelope. He opened it and read aloud to Kate.

"Carl with a 'C' N-a-s-s-o-n. Born December twenty-eight, nineteen forty-nine to John and Victoria Nasson of New York City, Saratoga Springs, Newport and San Francisco. Only child. Father inventor of a process of electrostatically painting extruded aluminum. Great wealth. Parents killed in crash of private plane over Acapulco in nineteen fifty-nine. Left everything to Carl. Closest living relative, an aunt, Amanda Gelamain of Manhattan. Carl graduated Manlius Academy and Harvard."

Casey handed Kate the folder with the photograph of Carl Nasson. She examined the angular features and vivid blue eyes. There was no doubt of the likeness to the brunette who had kidnapped Jenny.

"I need Amanda Gelamain's address," she said.

"We're already working on it," Casey said.

Hold on, Jenny.

CHAPTER FIFTY

"**P**LEASE tell us what you know," Kate said to Travers. Her lungs felt inadequate.

"First time I saw him I said to myself, I said, this guy would be a smash in Hollywood. I hope he's teachable. Coat-hanger shoulders, snake hips and an—"

He stared Casey down.

"—ass like a couple of hardballs bobbing in a pail of water."

Kate was proud of Casey for not making a gesture of any kind.

"But you must see a lot of handsome men in your profession," Kate said. "What made him so different?"

"He walked on ball bearings. Natural grace. Luminous blue eyes. Metallic. So comfortable in his own skin, own space, you couldn't keep from watching him. One of those rare ones who can be silent without disappearing."

Casey cleared his throat.

Kate said, "What kind of an actor, was he?"

"Like no one I ever met."

"That good?" Casey said.

"That strange. He was great at anything he was called

186

on to do alone. Super concentration. No one learned his lines as fast. Magic with costumes. Ask him to be a ripe apple about to fall or a mushroom growing in a cellar and no one could touch him. Not to be believed in certain monologues, soliloquies."

"What didn't he do well in?" Casey said.

"It was like he was always on stage by himself. Especially in love scenes. He'd go on and on but you'd swear he'd never felt it himself, which is ridiculous, but . . . it was almost as if . . . never mind, it's crazy."

"Something was missing?" Kate said.

"Exactly."

Kate and Casey waited.

"I always ask students to name their favorite actor of the opposite sex. Be surprised what you can learn. When it came to Carl I couldn't believe what I was hearing. Here's this gorgeous, sophisticated, bright . . . he chose this B movies actress from the forties, Lizabeth Scott."

"What was wrong with her?" Casey said.

Travers rolled his eyes.

A frustrating half light went on in Kate's head.

"For one, if Carl was listening, he would have known I was talking about the theater, not film. And if I'd asked for film people I would have expected at the time—sixties we're talking—a Hepburn or a Davis or a Bergman."

"Anything else?" Casey said.

"Once I cast him as Brick. You know, *Cat on a Hot Tin Roof.*"

"Yes," Kate said.

"Explained to him Maggie was burning with sexual frustration and trying to get him to fulfill his long neglected obligations in bed. But Carl kept getting hung up on her wanting to share his coming inheritance."

Kate said, "He quit after that, huh?"

"How did you know?"

"Gaelic intuition," Casey said.

"Another thing," Travers said. "His movements on stage were often inconsistent with his lines. To some extent that's true of all students. But this was . . . weird . . ."

Kate thought, I'm coming baby.

CHAPTER FIFTY-ONE

A T the Biarritz Cooperative on Fifth Avenue Kate stopped to examine the building where Nasson's aunt lived. A young woman emerged with a brace of miniature schnauzers. A Madison Avenue florist truck was double parked while the driver made deliveries. The liveried doorman doffed his hat when he closed a taxi door.

As she entered the lobby a gray-haired man in a flannel designer jogging outfit passed her. She recognized him from TV.

The doorman, a corpulent figure swelling importantly in gray and scarlet, greeted her. And, after calling upstairs for permission, rang the elevator for her.

At the designated floor Kate got off the elevator, making note that there were but two apartments.

She rang and a black maid had her wait in the foyer.

Amanda Gelamain finally appeared, trim and tan and stunning in beige britches tucked into black riding boots. Her cream silk blouse, opened wide at the throat, showed high, firm breasts.

The report Kate had gotten from Casey said Amanda

was sixty plus. Breast implants, no doubt. Yet the rest of her also looked impossibly young. Kate's eyes were trained on the woman's face. It wasn't her straight nose, high cheek bones, precision-cut hair like lamplight on wet tar, wide forehead or brown eyes wide as a painted doll's that amazed Kate. There were no age lines by the eyebrows, or crow's feet at the corners of the eyes. No extra flesh underneath the jaw. And her skin . . . like melted caramel.

There was no doubt about the face lift . . . or lifts.

Kate knew before she felt the extended hand it would be soft and warm. Never had she seen a more sultry woman.

"Sorry I couldn't see you sooner," Amanda Gelamain said in a husky voice which Kate thought suited her perfectly. "But I've been spending a ghastly amount of time with my attorneys lately over some silly business. They should spray for lawyers like they do mosquitoes."

Kate couldn't help smiling despite the seriousness of her visit.

"Please follow me," the older woman rasped.

Kate was led down a corridor the color of old port. In her wake Amanda left a lingering scent of dark and expensive perfume.

The living room smelled faintly of eucalyptus. It had a cathedral ceiling, Rafus palms in fine china pots in rows along the windowsills. A red marble fireplace. The armchairs were striped in maroon, walls papered in satins, curtains bone white, silver frames around prints of Rubenesque women reclining on blood red divans, pussy willows reaching out of charcoal vases. It was a room where one expected to hear the bright silver and honey sounds of a courtesan laughing.

"Coffee, tea, sherry, Scotch, Perrier?"

"Thank you, nothing."

"Excuse me, I'm going to get myself something."

She was of a color that seemed to absorb light. The room seemed brighter when she was out of sight.

Shortly she returned with an on-the-rocks glass three-quarters filled with what smelled like the bourbon Kate's father had drunk.

Amanda crossed her shapely legs and, offering Kate a cigarette from a silver box, took one herself.

Kate watched her light it seductively with a Dunhill table lighter.

"So," Amanda said, "shall we get down to it?"

"Please."

"Carl was always a problem."

"How do you mean?"

"Only child. Introvert. A girl's eyes and mouth. The strength of a panther. Very attached to his mother. Didn't care for my brother at all. Anyway, he was a tortured boy. Once we—my brother—caught him throwing a cat into a furnace."

Typical, Kate thought, excited.

"Strangely," Amanda went on, "when he was growing up he wasn't interested much in girls."

"Forgive me, I appreciate this but—"

"Where can you find him?"

"Right."

"I wish I could tell you."

"When was the last time you saw him?"

"I don't remember. He was very young. A boy. We had gotten a complaint from his biology teacher about his killing too many frogs."

"Yes . . . has he been an actor?"

"As a matter of fact, he was a member of an acting school."

"Name?"

"I forget. Long time ago."

"I see. And how would you describe Carl's relationship with your sister-in-law?"

"Very close. Some people thought too close. My brother was quite jealous of it."

Kate thought she saw a flicker of regret in Amanda's expression.

"Did your sister-in-law smoke?"

"I beg your pardon?"

"Some complicated forensics. I'm not even sure I understand it myself."

"Alberta didn't smoke or drink. Sure you won't have something?"

Kate read the dismissal in the tone, but ignored it. "Is there anyone else you'd recommend my contacting?"

"His schools, of course."

"Of course," she said, and continued to question her . . .

Outside Kate stood appreciating the fresh cold air as she waited to hail a taxi. How deliberately Amanda volunteered information: *Only child. Introvert. Very attached to his mother. Some people thought too close.* She claimed she hadn't seen him since he was very young, but knew he had taken lessons at an acting studio for adults. Made a point of saying he had killed a cat and frogs, acts characteristic of serial killers when growing up.

Kate wasn't positive, but a lot of the signs were there. Could it have been the aunt, not the mother?

As they sat in the kind of pub Casey referred to as a "hothouse gin mill" because of all the hanging plants, Kate suddenly said, *I've got it!"*

Casey saw that an old familiar light was on again in Kate's eyes. "C'mon! C'mon!"

"Lizabeth Scott and Lauren Bacall and Amanda Ge-lamain."

"What? I'm dying here."

"The voice I told you his aunt has."

"Yeah?"

"Of course. We couldn't see the connection with all the victims. They were dead. They were silenced."

"Keep going."

"I think if you check, you'll find all the victims had a husky Lauren Bacall voice."

"I can always count on you, Katie dear." He leaned over and kissed her cheek. "God bless your Gaelic heart and your Yiddish head!"

I'm coming, baby.

CHAPTER FIFTY-TWO

WHEN Jenny woke she could taste blood on her gums and feel how swollen her lip was. One tooth was loose.

She wept, out of control.

She didn't know for how long she cried. She managed to get to the bathroom. The mirror was gone. He had punished her by taking away the companionship of her reflection. What else had he done? She sneezed. Must be coming down with a cold from being outside in the snow and rain.

Back in her room she saw that he had removed all the cassette tapes and the recorder, all books, even her writing paper and pencil. She shook, feeling his anger.

She heard the door open. His eyes were awful.

When she found her voice she said, "What are you going to do with me?" As soon as she spoke she regretted her words.

"Don't you like suspense?"

"I'm sorry. It wasn't personal. You can't blame me for wanting to be free, can you?"

"I do blame you. I trusted you. You betrayed me."

The hatred in his tone struck her like a blow. Her lip quivered. She tried to acquire a cool look, but her stomach threatened to spill itself.

In one violently quick movement he was upon her and his hand had slapped her face.

"Please, I'll do whatever you want."

"Naturally."

His certainty unnerved her still further.

This couldn't be happening. Any moment she would be invited to lie on a blanket on a fine summer night and watch for shooting stars with Uncle Josh and Aunt Kate.

She heard a slight metallic sound.

"It's time for retribution," he said.

He was holding a switchblade in his hand. It felt like the weight of the entire room was on her chest.

"Oh God, please, I'll do anything. You just tell me. I didn't realize . . ."

The metal was ice against her skin. What had she done that God should ignore her so?

She tried to breath. Fear gripped her lungs.

"I s-wear I'll never ask to go outside again. Ever."

The slap rattled her head. She fought to stay conscious.

"When are you going to learn I'm the only one who has control of your fate?"

It took her a moment to realize she'd been asked a question.

"I've learned it now."

The air rushed out of her in a sob.

He was hovering over her. She was gasping.

"Please, God."

"Don't pray."

"S-sure, okay. Anything you say, only please—"

"Don't beg."

She heard nothing except his excited breathing. His stare met hers. She could feel herself dissolving.

"Maybe I should pay you back with a hysterectomy."
She bit a piece of the inside of her cheek.
Then he rose.
"Don't ever betray me again."
When he left she lay like some puny animal struggling
helplessly to escape its pain.

CHAPTER FIFTY-THREE

ALL day Kate and Josh had waited while the phone grew and grew with the urge to ring but didn't. Josh could hear himself breathing. Kate felt her eyes getting hot.

When Casey arrived at 4:18 he said to Josh, "We're working on the voice theory. Find anything out?"

Josh spoke in a faraway voice. "The story almost never varied at Nasson's prep school and at Harvard. An unusually brilliant student, great athlete, loner. Caught throwing a cat into one of the school furnaces.

"Until I tracked down that girl he dated in college. Lisa Merton. Must've put on fifty pounds since her graduation picture. A pink woman inside a tent of a housecoat. She told me she'd stopped seeing him because of his incendiary temper, but she continued to get letters from him. Even when she changed addresses and jobs, he always found out where she was. Finally, after many years, he lost interest."

"Or found other interests," Casey said.

Josh continued, "She said she loves her husband but

Nasson had really gotten to her. Scared hell out of her, but maybe that was what the big turn-on was."

"Reminds me," Casey said, "of all those women used to sit in the courtroom when Bundy was being tried. They'd iron their hair straight and part it down the middle like they'd read in the papers he liked and stare into his eyes till he looked back at them. Even married one in a court- room while he was on trial. Had a kid with her. Gives me the willies."

"Thank God the kid was a girl," Josh said.

Kate was faraway in her thoughts. Someone like Bundy had her little girl.

CHAPTER FIFTY-FOUR

"**T**HIS just isn't working," Kate said to Josh and Casey in the living room of the detective's home in New Rochelle.

Casey shot out of his plaid La-Z-Boy almost spilling his Old Fashioned on Molly McGee. "Tell me about it. Now we know who he is and why he chooses certain women. So now what do we do?"

Josh said, "At his prep school and Harvard a couple of people kept saying, 'Must be the wrong guy.' "

"Yeah," Casey said, "like Bundy couldn't have worked a suicide hotline and done all those college kids. But he did. Take your drinks, I want to show you something."

He led them down a corridor cluttered with plastic-framed photographs. Here was Casey being decorated by Mayor Lindsay. Casey and wife Moira posing in front of a lifeboat inscribed Spring Lake. A Police Athletic League plaque. Casey and Moira surrounded by children and grandchildren under a banner reading: CASEY-McNAB CLANS CLAM BAKE 1978. No new ones, Kate noticed.

They entered his den. The walls were knotty pine, something Kate hadn't seen in a home since the fifties, except his. Artificial brick fireplace. Oil painting of John Kennedy above it. Bar with four Naugahyde stools. To the right of the bar the entire wall was covered with photographs and drawings connected with red magic marker lines.

Kate and Josh looked at each other, then examined the wall more closely.

There were 8 by 10s of Nasson's victims, drawings or photographs of the weapons, dates and times of each crime, etcetera.

He moved his office home as he always does with a big case, Kate thought. She could see fresh Scotch tape marks in a place where Toby's photograph had been. She was grateful Casey had removed it.

"As you can see, what I don't know takes up the biggest space," Casey said. "Let me get you guys another drink."

They begged off, but Casey fixed himself another.

The three sat silently for a time. Then Kate, with a look in her eye both recognized, began, "Tracing down all our leads we're undoubtedly only going to learn how and why he got the way he is. Which is secondary now."

"Not even that," Casey said.

"We have to work with what we already know about him and other psychopaths to smoke him out."

"Okay," Casey said, putting his glass down and resuming his pacing. "Smart, rich, strong, careful."

"But what are his weaknesses?" Kate said.

"He cares more about revenge than his safety," Casey said.

"Cigar," Kate said.

Josh said, "He got insanely insulted with the piece in the *National Exposé*."

"Exactly," Kate said.

"So?" Casey said.

"So," Kate went on, "we pin murders on him in the

paper. We make up letters he supposedly wrote to the paper."

Casey said, "A phony copycat killer—beautiful!"

"Brilliant!" said Josh.

"Here's my plan . . ." Kate said.

CHAPTER FIFTY-FIVE

SERIAL KILLER STRIKES AGAIN!

Mrs. Christine Keller of 105-40 Yellowstone Boulevard appears to be the latest victim of the serial killer terrorizing our city.

Police say the murder happened early yesterday morning when the killer broke into Mrs. Keller's apartment in a large garden apartment building in the Forest Hills section of Queens. Mrs. Keller was in the process of moving in.

The body was found by a tenant. One police officer said, "Looked like the poor lady backed into a buzz saw."

Forensic units from the Medical Examiner's office are still combing the site.

SERIAL SLAYER RETURNS!

Third attack in a week indicates quickening of killer's activity.

202

MULTIPLE KILLER NEARLY CAUGHT!

LETTER TO THE EDITOR
FROM THE SERIAL KILLER

I am the personification of The Demon Lover. The hero of risk. A living weapon. I excite with the thrill of fear. Women lust to have me. Men lust to be me. A hundred years ago I would have been considered a freak. Now, there are dozens, hundreds of me. Soon there'll be thousands. And I'll be considered an amateur.

Nasson threw down the clippings. How he'd love to know the name of the punk who had the gall to imitate him. As if he could be imitated by anyone. His brain accelerated with ideas about how to obliterate the upstart.

Without warning, years compressed in his thoughts and a moment from the past crystallized.

Embrace me, my sweet embraceable you . . .

The black flower of Her voice festooned: low, dusty, lacy, dark, throbbing, deadly.

She took his hand and placed it on her soft, breathing belly. The satin was softer than any skin. His breathing became the same as hers. She drew his head down to where her hairs lifted her slip just the slightest. Her perfume stopped him, then spun, twirled and left him dizzy.

He had breathed so hard that he was afraid his chest would break. He pulled away. She held him in her soft

203

lotioned hands and pointed to his rigid little thing sticking straight out, hurtful in its hardness.

When she rubbed the cool lotion between his legs his breath, sight, hearing stopped.

"Stop it, please," he cried. "I'm so scared."

She stroked him with just the tips of her fingers. Moved gently with her nails. He grew dizzy.

. . . my irreplaceable you . . .

He couldn't breathe. Felt as if he were being pulled away even as he was drawn toward her warmth, her slickness, her scent.

She moved so her velvet belly brushed him where he ached.

"I wish you wouldn't, please," he whispered.

"I know, dear, but it feels good, doesn't it?"

"Yes, but—Ohhh!"

Her tongue ran along his little length.

Up and down and around.

His belly did little jumps. Could he die?

"Ummmm"

It was more a gravel in her throat than a vocal sound.

Time expanded and he was suspended between the part of himself that refused to lose control and the part that was lost in the moment.

"Oh," he said, unaware that his voice had changed.

And he gave himself up to that dark, warm, moist space in which there was nothing except her mouth and him.

Later, he went to his mother to tell.

Her slap still seared his face.

"Don't ever let me hear *one* word about your Aunt Amanda again. No one in our family would ever *think* of doing such a thing. Never. People in our family have never been that *interested* in sex. *Now* take your pants down and take your punishment like a *man.*"

"Not even that interested," he said, now.

Hate lay so heavily on his tongue it churned his stomach. He ran to the toilet.

CHAPTER FIFTY-SIX

NASSON, dressed as a mailman, was crouching on a roof two streets away from the building on Yellowstone Boulevard where Christine Keller was killed by his impersonator. There were no police barricades but he was sure, looking through his binoculars, that the two men in the nondescript Chevy must be cops. If his imitator did return to the scene he would have to deal with the cops as well as with him.

He smiled. He knew another way to stop this imposter.

The phone rang.

Kate let the silence grow on the line till her ears pounded with blood.

"Yes, who is this?"

"Now, really. You know who."

The night poured its silence and darkness into her anticipation.

Her skin felt like metal, her heart drummed against it.

She managed to dredge up, "It's you."

"What gave you the first clue?"

"Please, is Jenny okay?"

"I'll prove to you she is if you'll trade. All right?"

"All right."

"Good. I never sent those stupid letters to the newspapers and I never killed those last three."

"What do you want?"

"I want a statement in the papers tomorrow afternoon or else the New Year's going to ring in without your niece in it. Understand?"

"I understand. Now prove to me Jenny's all right."

"She'll tell you herself. Make it quick. Before the trace." Good thing he hadn't finished her. He'd had the feeling since he first took her she'd be useful to him somehow.

"I'm okay, Aunt Kate."

Thank you, God. "You sound sick."

"It's nothing. A cold."

"We love you, darling. Do what he says! And if you get a hoarse throat, whisper—he might hear you."

"What? I—"

"That's enough," Nasson said. "Tomorrow afternoon. Happy New Year."

Click.

Kate watched herself stagger over and collapse into a chair, the air around her head warm and cottony.

Alive. The chambers of her heart were filled with exaltation and relief.

She picked up the receiver and punched Josh's office number. Jenny had sounded a bit nasal and chesty. She could have pneumonia, for all anybody knew.

Please hold on, baby.

God, don't let her cold reach her throat.

CHAPTER FIFTY-SEVEN

SERIAL KILLER HAS COPYCAT!

*New York City Chief of Detectives Bill Casey disclosed
last night at a press conference that evidence shows that
the last three killings alleged to be that of the serial killer
were committed by a copycat. Chief Casey said the letters,
reportedly sent to this newspaper and others by the killer
were also the work of a copycat.*

Kate slammed the newspaper down on the massive
desk of the Chief.

Josh and Casey exchanged a helpless look.

Kate went over to the window and looked down at the
orange brick structure that is One Police Plaza. The noise
of traffic reached up and penetrated the room.

Casey said, "I should've known I couldn't get away
forever with having an office on the thirteenth floor. One
flight up the Commissioner's sitting behind Teddy
Roosevelt's desk scheming how he can make me a meter
maid. Sorry, Katie, I know my problems are shit next—"

"Problems are problems," she said.

"Where do we go from here?" Josh said.

"We go back to the basics," Kate said. "Contrary to what I thought at the very beginning, he does care what people think of him. He is interested in what's in the newspapers."

"Keep going," Casey said.

"We got to him beautifully with phony newspaper stories, right?" Kate said.

"Right," Casey said.

"So?" said Josh.

"So we plant another story," Kate said. "But this time we hit him where he's most vulnerable. A woman with a voice like Lauren Bacall."

"Bait," Casey said.

"Exactly." Kate said. "An Elizabeth Ashley or Brenda Vaccaro, and those are only two. How about Joni Freemont?"

Casey said, "What makes you think one of the top singers in the country is going to let us use her as bait?"

"Because," Josh said, "Kate has done an awful lot for her daughter Lilah. She has autism."

There was a buzz on the intercom.

"Yes?" Casey said. Pause. "Well tell the Commissioner I already left, Lieutenant." Pause. "Then tell him you made a mistake before you really make one." He turned to them. "I can't think with the Commissioner pacing over my head. C'mon, we got to eat, anyway." He rose.

"Eat?" Kate said. "My baby's got a cold, could develop into a hoarse throat and we're going to eat?"

"We'll drink," Casey said. "We'll talk. We'll figure it out."

Dunne's was one of the few remaining authentic Irish taverns in Manhattan. Real mahogany bar. The bartender wore sleeve garters, a bow tie and an apron. He served their drinks on an ancient tray bearing the face of a former Miss Rheingold.

The three of them sat in a leather booth, their drinks on Guiness coasters.

Casey said, "Really think Joni Freemont'll do it?"

"We've got an appointment at her place in less than an hour," Kate said.

"You're a fast woman." Casey lifted a sweating bottle of ale.

"No, a desperate one," she pulled the near-empty bowl of salted peanuts away from Josh, who had unconsciously been trying to eat his way out of anxiety.

CHAPTER FIFTY-EIGHT

A maid met them at the door of Joni Freemont's penthouse that overlooked Central Park. She led them down a corridor whose walls were covered with gold and platinum records and framed photographs of Miss Freemont with Michael Jackson, Frank Sinatra and Mikhail Gorbachev.

Kate had rarely seen Casey awed. Especially by the decor of rooms in which he had little interest. He put his lips together as if to whistle and only blew out air.

A six-paneled gold-and-black Japanese screen depicting a peaceful scene of mountains and trees dominated one hunter green wall. Black delft jar lamps stood on Chinese lacquered cabinets bracketing the mauve sofa. Against another wall was a black grand piano. The furniture nested on a turn-of-the-century Persian carpet, except for the piano, which was on glistening wood flooring.

The room was lit by muted lamplight and the flames from a black marble fireplace which reflected on yellow Enchantment lilies, leaves of bamboo trees, netsuke and Zen brush paintings of shore reeds. It was peaceful as well as elegant.

When Joni Freemont entered in a raspberry pullover and black velvet slacks, her poise and charming smile were as organic to the surroundings as jade and ivory.

After Joni and Kate hugged and Casey shook the singer's hand, they sat in rosewood chairs around the fire.

There was very little speech but no awkward pauses or silences. Joni poured sherry for each of them without asking. Her irises were the color of the wine. But once more Kate was struck by how her bitter divorce and, even more important, Lilah's having autism, had left her eyes sad and lusterless.

A white Persian cat slinked into the room and jumped onto Joni's lap.

"How can I help you?" Joni said in her deep and throaty voice.

"I would never ask you this," Kate said, "if I knew any other way."

"Kate, please go on."

"Whatever we've tried with this bastard who has Jenny hasn't worked. He let me speak to her on the phone. She's got a cold. Whenever she gets a cold she gets a hoarse throat. As you know, what all the victim's have in common is a voice similar to yours."

"Here," Joni said, "let me open a window, get some air in here."

She poured the cat off her lap.

"Thanks, I'm okay. To be blunt—we need a decoy."

"I see," Joni said, in a quiet tone.

She walked over to the window and stared out at the Park.

The three waited, eager for the singer's response.

Joni turned to face them. "For years I tried to help Lilah on my own. Nearly killed myself trying. I'd watch *The Miracle Worker* till I could recite the lines. Then you came to the institute, Kate, and Jenny came into Lilah's life. Her first friend . . . I'm scared, I don't mind telling you, but maybe I can help win this one. At least this gives me something tangible to fight. Let's say I owe you and Jenny one. One, two, three, as high as I can count."

Kate's heart expanded in her chest.

Josh and Casey turned to Kate. She was walking across the room toward Joni, arms outstretched.

CHAPTER FIFTY-NINE

". . . I refuse to change even one of my plans because of that monster . . ." Joni Freemont said to one of the reporters gathered in her living room.

Nasson, watching the much publicized press conference, smashed his fist down on a table. She had the voice, and she had dared to call him that!

"Damn, that woman's good!" Casey said. He and Kate and Josh sat huddled before the Sony in the Berman den.

"Last week I decided to take a few days off to visit with my daughter, who's at an institute for kids with autism in Rhinebeck. I have a house there in the woods where I go as a kind of retreat. People kept saying to me, 'You should be hiding, with your voice. Especially since the aunt of the girl he kidnapped works at your daughter's institute.' "

The singer's living room crackled with energy and conjecture.

Nasson finished his Scotch, poured another and drained that one too.

". . . I didn't go. But I'm going now. I'm going because

no lunatic is going to keep me from seeing my daughter . . ."

The room filled with applause.

Nasson began to tremble from the hate steaming out of him.

Kate said, "Terrific lady."

". . . I'm going because I know there are women singers, actors, housewives in this city who haven't left their homes since the police told us this despicable creature's victims all had voices like mine . . ."

Nasson's pupils had gotten so large his sight was blurry.

". . . Well I say it's time we women took a stand against this freak . . ."

Nasson shot from his chair.

"How do you propose that be done, Joni?" called a reporter Kate recognized from the eleven o'clock news on NBC.

"By ignoring this monster. Going on as usual."

Josh said, "Is she terrific, or what?"

Blood massed in Nasson's throat. *This one,* he said to Her, *will suffer* so much, *she'll beg me to take her life.*

A woman in a tailored pin-striped suit called out to Joni, "Is that what you advise the women in our city to do?"

"I'm not qualified to advise anyone else. I just hope that my telling them how I refuse to let this pig change my lifestyle will help other women."

The veins in Nasson's neck had risen and showed blue.

"Do you expect to see Dr. Kate Berman while you're upstate?" a reporter shouted.

"Absolutely."

Nasson brought his glass down on the table so hard it splintered in his hand. He never took his eyes off the screen.

"Only hope the bastard is watching," Josh said.

"If not," Casey said, "this'll be front page."

". . . that's about it, ladies and gentlemen. Thank you for coming."

Nasson didn't wait for the applause. It would mock him even more. He pressed the remote control button.

He went to the kitchen, opened the faucet and put his head under the wet cold till he shook. Took huge drafts of water which hurt his throat where the blood was still collected. Returned to his chair in the living room and sat focusing his mind on what he must do now.

First he had to find out where in Rhinebeck she lived.

A thought occurred to him that made the muscles in his face relax. He was smiling.

This one had done him a favor. After he had punished her he would take care of Kate Berman. Her husband, too. And, of course, the girl in the next room.

Watch me! he said to Her.

CHAPTER SIXTY

I don't have any paper or pencil so I can only write in my head.

I wish I knew what Aunt Kate meant when she said, "Whisper, he might hear you." If I do, he will *hear me.*

I've always loved God but now I don't know. If he's good how could he have made this man?

I'm so sick. Temperature, aches, nose, head, chest, throat. The same order a cold always takes with me. My mouth and lip still hurt where he hit me. Thank God he didn't . . .

What kind of God lets babies starve in Africa? People being tortured in South Korea? Women like me kept prisoner by men like him?

Whisper, he might hear you. . . .

Why was Aunt Kate afraid of his hearing my normal voice? No, not my normal voice. The voice I have when I get a cold . . . a hoarse voice . . .

I'm so scared. More than I've ever been. My head is burning up. Maybe I've got pneumonia, and I'll die before he can kill me. God, this is the worst. No one will even know when I die. Except Uncle Josh. He'll know when they find me.

I can't stand thinking like this anymore. Shaking. I'm not going to die. I won't. I'm too young. I have just as much right as anyone. My throat hurts so much I can't swallow. A hoarse voice . . .

I'm losing my mind. Need to keep the light on all the time. I keep thinking what he'll do to me—after. I shouldn't care—I won't feel it—but I do.

I won't stop living.

Oh God, I'm sorry to doubt you. I'm just so scared. Please, don't let him. Make me wake up in my room at home. Anywhere but here.

I can't take any more.

Make him stop.

Please.

CHAPTER SIXTY-ONE

NASSON awoke at dawn, coughing and choking. He had bitten through his pillow and his mouth was filled with goose down. *I must have another soon,* he told Her.

Dressed in black watch cap over red hair, jeans and a ski jacket, he took a private taxi service to a used car dealer right off the George Washington Bridge in Fort Lee, New Jersey.

He scanned the lot and chose a dark gray two-door Chevy. The sale tag said $4,995.

A salesman who wore a slightly askew hairpiece took a Hav A Tampa out of his mouth and crooned, "Cream, real cream." His eyes were like spoiled cherries.

Nasson peered inside the car ignoring the odometer's false reading of less than twenty thousand miles.

"Never had an accident," the salesman said, looking him over.

"Have you got the title?"

"Right in the office."

He showed the salesman a roll of hundreds. Then, careful not to look too eager, he said, "I'll give you four thousand dollars."

"Forty-five hundred and I pay the tax."

"I'll drive it out."

He told the salesman his name was Richard Kohler. With the cash on the desk he wasn't asked for identification. He signed a statement saying he had insurance.

Are You watching so far?

Nasson drove along the Taconic Parkway toward Rhinebeck. He was dressed as a priest, and wore a black wig and rimless bifocals. His mind was focused on the problem of how to get Joni Freemont and the Bermans together, kill them and escape. And what disguise would be best under the circumstances.

With all the publicity, he felt sure the singer's country home was being watched by the police. And the Bermans always had that moronic Chief of Detectives around.

The institute for kids with autism was the obvious choice. It had so many people going in and out that he would be less noticeable.

Then the matter of choosing a disguise. He knew physical disguises—a wig, a beard—were usually a cover-up designed to make the wearer unrecognizable. They didn't really camouflage the wearer. They could, in fact, make him stand out in a crowd.

The art of psychological disguise, on the other hand, lies in the ability to make oneself blend into the surroundings so that he cannot be seen as a separate entity. To become invisible.

Nasson knew that non-being was a state of mind. Everyone practiced it at times, to avoid someone in order not to be noticed.

Years ago, when he lived in San Francisco he had often

boarded the cable car wearing a raincoat of indeterminate age and color which helped to put him in the right mood. He made himself small, averting his eyes and imagining he was somewhere else. The conductor always passed him by, never once asking for his fare.

He enjoyed being able to quiet his mind at will so that his presence couldn't be felt.

He knew that people saw strangers as stereotypes. All Orientals really looked alike to many Caucasians, just as many Orientals thought all Caucasians looked alike.

Therefore, fitting other people's preconceptions was an excellent disguise because those readily classified as types became invisible. People saw what they expected to see.

There were, however, stereotypes that were highly visible because they were threatening, like police or vagrants. Non-threatening types were servants, waitresses, gas station attendants, mailmen and UPS men. The list was endless.

He decided to use the guise of a Federal Express man because the same UPS man probably visited the Institute on a daily basis. Federal Express rarely had a daily pickup, because UPS was cheaper. He could store the priest's clothing in his valise.

When he combined his skill of non-being with the invisibility of a Federal Express uniform he would be as overlooked as a chameleon in a bed of leaves.

For the rest of the trip he perfected his plan.

Nasson parked the sedan in the parking lot of Rhinebeck's Beekman Arms ("Oldest Inn in America"), where it wouldn't draw suspicion if it remained hour after hour.

He asked at the front desk where the Institute was. Luckily, it was only one block away. Blessed small towns.

He walked there and saw a large Tudor-like structure set in from the main road.

Once there he asked where the Federal Express drop box was located. Hearing it was only two streets away in a mini shopping mall, he smiled. Everything was going perfectly.

The sign on the drop box said pickups were at three P.M. He bought a map at the Rhinebeck Smoke Shop.

Having a sandwich in Schemmy's Ice Cream Parlor, he pretended to be reading a leather bound Bible with a bishop-blue silk bookmark. Instead, he was concentrating on his state of non-being. Clearing his mind, remaining calm and confident. Not arousing suspicion by making noise, taking up too much space, or moving quickly (unless, of course, circumstances dictated otherwise).

Perhaps most important was to remember to avoid eye contact. As a student of martial arts he had been taught to avoid eye contact and staring at opponents, even when behind them. He had learned that people intuitively sensed scrutiny and would instinctively turn to see who was staring at them.

At six minutes to three he paid his check, leaving neither too small nor too large a tip, put his Bible in his black valise and went to the Federal Express drop box.

Helping himself to supplies from the box he filled out an air bill using a fictitious party and address.

At precisely three, a Federal Express truck pulled up.

"Hi ya, Father, got something for me?"

The driver had twenty pounds on him but such uniforms were not expected to be well tailored.

"Why don't you empty the box, I'll only be a minute or so."

Soon the driver said, "Ready, Father?" and stepped into the cab of his truck.

Nasson walked over to the driver's window and handed the man an overnight letter pouch.

"Thank you, Father."

Nasson reached in, patted the driver's shoulder. Maneuvered the blade up between his fingers and pressed it against the man's jugular. "One word and you're dog food."

"I . . . whatever you want . . ."

"I want you to move over slowly, calmly, to the passenger's side. Then I'm going to get in behind the wheel as if I'm looking for something I dropped on the floor. Got it so far?"

"Y-yes, but—"

"I'm not finished. Then I'll make believe I found my key and we'll both smile and you'll climb over me to the driver's seat. Start doing what I just went through."

In moments the driver's assignment was completed.

"Good," Nasson said, pulling a map from the inside pocket of his jacket. "Now get over to Ferncliff Forest on Mt. Rutsen Road. Don't speed. Smile."

Nasson had discovered Ferncliff when investigating the area around the Valeur Mansion. The forest was a preserved area.

When they arrived at Ferncliff the driver said, "What now?"

"Now this," Nasson said delivering a rabbit punch to the back of his neck. The blow killed him instantly.

"Thanks for a wonderful evening. Let's do it again some time."

Nasson dragged the driver's corpse into the forest, removed the uniform, and buried the body under the snow, brush and branches.

He returned to the truck and placed the uniform in his valise. Dressed as a priest again.

Then he drove the truck deep into the woods. It was

223

nearly four P.M. and already getting dark. Who would look for a truck in the woods after dark?

By morning he would already have executed his plan and gone. *Do You see how precise I am?*

Now for Joni Freemont's and the Bermans' surprise.

CHAPTER SIXTY-TWO

W HEN Knox "Boomer" Elmendorf, Captain of the Bureau of Criminal Investigation, shouted, "Listen up," there was an immediate hush in the garage of the Rhinebeck trooper barracks.

There was so much brass and so many troopers and New York City detectives involved that they had been in a quandry about whether to hold the briefing at the much larger facility in Millbrook about thirty miles away. Finally the brass decided on the Rhinebeck barracks garage, a gray cinder-block building with a single window and a generator the size of a small tractor.

To accommodate all the troopers, BCI investigators, Mobile Response Teams, brass from division headquarters in Albany, and Casey's men, there was standing room only. The New York City detectives looked out of focus, tired from overtime.

Knox was a tall, straight, greyhound of a man whose military bearing lent his presence weight. His dishwater eyes spoke of a cynicism accumulated during a long, up-from-the-ranks police career.

There was no need to tell his fellow officers of the seriousness of the briefing. All days off and vacations had been canceled. Rarely did the captain give a briefing, and then only at headquarters. Besides, they had read the papers. They could plainly see that Chief Casey was present.

"You know why you're here," Knox began in his booming voice, "but you don't know all of it, so listen up. We believe that Nasson is here in Rhinebeck. He's after Joni Freemont and probably Kate and Josh Berman, too. Each of these people is wearing a beeper. Surveillance couldn't be tighter. That's not the problem.

"Contrary to what the media says or what's happened in the past, this is one time there'll be total cooperation between different law enforcement agencies. For that reason I'm going to let Chief Casey brief you on the rest. Anything the Chief says is to be taken as a direct order from me. Chief?"

Casey nodded then turned to the others. He had lost weight, looked drawn.

"Thank you, Captain," he said. "The problem is that this degenerate has a nineteen-year-old girl hidden somewhere in New York City. She could be anywhere, and there's a chance if he doesn't lead us to her she could die of starvation or dehydration."

Heads nodded.

"We need this guy alive. And I say this with the Captain's full agreement—only use deadly physical force as a last resort.

"Ideally we want to stop this guy from hurting Joni Freemont or the Bermans, scare him off, and be on him when he goes back to where he's hiding the girl.

"Nasson is not crazy in the sense that he's out of control. He's aware of everything that he's doing and what the penalties are. He makes plans. Involved, intricate ones. He's used all kinds of disguises. An old blind man, an elevator repairman, even a woman.

"Between troopers, the sheriff's office and my own people we have a net that covers every possible road from here back to the city, or anyplace else he tries to escape."

Someone coughed.

"Each of you will be given more explicit instructions by your immediate superiors. Remember, this freak is the only priority. We're going to pass out pictures of him. Then let's do it!"

CHAPTER SIXTY-THREE

Two drivers pulled up to him on his walk back to town and asked if he needed a lift.

"Only exercise I get, thank you," he assured both in a resolutely matter-of-fact voice. "God bless you."

When he reached town it was nearly four-thirty. Perfect.

He went to the men's room in the Beekman Arms, concentrating on non-being. In one of the stalls he changed into the Federal Express uniform.

Leaving by a door other than the one he had used to enter the hotel, he went round to the parking lot and threw the black valise in back of the car.

He walked the one block back to the Institute. People would assume he had parked his truck a short distance away.

At the front door he took a deep breath. He was never so alive as during a stalk. Everything from evergreens to a discarded gum wrapper sprang into crystal clear focus.

Inside, the disinfectant smell and the pale green walls reminded him of a hospital.

Behind a receptionist's desk sat a middle-aged woman with the ingratiating manner of a restaurant hostess.

"May I help you?" she said in a musical tone.

Optimists in small towns.

"Please. I'm looking for a Rosamund Kupner." The name of the first one he had chosen, in San Francisco. It was good luck. Besides, no chance of another by that name here. He wondered if She remembered.

"No Kupner works here. I can tell you that."

"Couldn't be for one of the patients?"

"A few of our residents do get mail, but there's none by that name either. I've been here for eighteen years."

My condolences, he thought.

"These things happen more and more nowadays. Mind if I use the rest room, ma'am?"

"Right around the corner there, to your right. Is John sick?"

John? Of course. "Yes, he's got the flu."

"Shame."

"Thanks again."

He had done it.

He padded away, feeling the power rising in him.

The bathroom smelled of mop water. He went inside a stall and relieved himself. In less than eight minutes it would be five o'clock, and the administrative staff would be going home.

After dinner the kitchen staff would undoubtedly leave. The place would be left with only a skeleton crew.

Then he would find the office where Kate Berman worked, and where the singer and her daughter were most likely to meet.

He settled himself comfortably on the seat and brought his legs under him.

With his malevolent grin he looked like a gargoyle just come to life.

Embrace me, my sweet embraceable you . . .

Suddenly there was blue television light. He saw himself as a boy watching *Walt Disney World* on a Sunday night with the family. Aunt Amanda sat next to him on the couch. When she placed the cushion in his lap he knew. He was afraid Mom and Dad might see, feel how excited he was. And scared. And guilty. He hated her for making him feel he was bad. What she made him feel was wrong. But he loved her too. She made him feel special. Important. Because she was the only one who paid attention to him.

Oh! He felt her smooth, warm hands pulling on his thing now under the cushion. So good. Then her hot tongue in his ear. It felt funny and he was scared. But it also felt good. The good feeling was in him so it had to be his fault. So ashamed. He had tried telling his mother but she didn't believe him.

His thing was so solid now it hurt. When it started to feel extra good Aunt Amanda knew and she bit his ear harder and harder. He wanted to yell but he couldn't and that made it feel even better in some way he didn't understand. He felt good and bad then at the same time and it made him afraid. Afraid and mad.

After a while the other feelings went away. But not the mad. The mad never went away. Never.

Now Nasson shifted his weight on the seat feeling the anger. He tried to think of nothing at all. But his thoughts soon returned to a golden afternoon when he was thirteen batting some baseballs. He had fallen asleep on the grass in the park near his house.

Without warning he was startled out of his sleep by the snapping of teeth at his face. Two weird, huge, yellow eyes were right in front of him. Then he saw the teeth and he knew it was a dog.

When the teeth grabbed at his leg he screamed and reached for his bat. Swung it down on the furry head. A yelp. What an exciting feeling the contact gave him! He swung again. The dog was flung to the ground on its side, blood gushing from its coral-shell ear.

The excitement localized in his groin. Drawn closer by the sight of the blood, he raised the bat again and brought it down on the eye. He felt himself grow hard between his legs.

He brought the bat down again and again till his underwear was wet and sticky. He felt filled. Loving.

Nasson's right leg cramped so he had to clasp his palm over his mouth to keep from crying out. He threw his leg straight out. As he rubbed the muscle he said to Her, *Watch what I do next!*

CHAPTER SIXTY-FOUR

JENNY shivered despite her fever. Burning up.

Where was he? Was he ever coming back? She wasn't hungry, but she missed the familiarity and comfort of food. Not having eaten in so long was probably making her weaker.

Too weak to move. But she had to have water when she had a fever.

"Liquids," Dr. Siegel from the city used to say when she and Kate and Josh lived there. Oh to have his big, soft, gentle hands patting her head as he said, "If I give you medicine this cold or flu or whatever you want to call it will take a week to run its course. Otherwise it'll take seven days."

She wept at the old joke between the kind doctor and her family.

If only it was just a cold. But if he didn't come back . . . if he'd just left her here to die—what difference did it make?

She pulled herself from the bed. These legs weren't hers. They must've gotten confused with someone else's. These were old, weak, brittle, trembling.

232

"Mother of God, please."

Grasping the wall she made her way tentatively toward the bathroom.

When she turned on the basin faucet her legs gave out and she sat on the lip of the tub pouring cool water onto her face and neck. Shivered with the cold. But it felt good. Except for the pain when the cold hit the nerve of her loose tooth.

She watched her hand scoop liquid into her mouth, rinse then swallow.

Like pebbles on her sore throat. Sore throat. Hoarse voice. *Whisper, he might hear you* . . . what had Aunt Kate meant?

She couldn't remember ever having wanted to see someone more than she wanted him to return. At least then it might all be over quickly.

The thought twisted her bowel. She pulled herself over to the commode and sat eliminating a watery, odorless substance.

Feed a cold? Starve a fever? She couldn't remember.

She wasn't going to die. She remembered that people could live for a long time without food, as long as they had water.

She would drown the fever. Rest in bed. Pray. Think of Aunt Kate and Uncle Josh. Ginny. College. Maybe she wouldn't transfer. People were the same everywhere.

Whisper, he might hear you. What had Aunt Kate meant? She had never even considered dying this young, except when Robbie showed off driving too fast and she had had to threaten to get out at the first traffic light if he didn't slow down.

She thought of Grandpa Duffy. Aunt Kate's face with gray hair and eyebrows so thick they looked like bunting.

"You got Irish cop blood in you, darling. Things get tough, just remember to keep punching."

Her thoughts settled her stomach. She wiped, flushed, stood to wash her hands.

There was only a sliver of soap left. *Keep punching.*

Wait! A hoarse throat. Aunt Kate must've found out that all the women had a hoarse voice! That's it!

When he returned she had to remember not to speak. Whisper . . .

She dropped the soap and it fell to the floor. She bent down to get it. When she rose the blood left her head, and the room spun away from her. She grasped the porcelain of the sink. Then she clutched at the aluminum support rods underneath.

The lip of the tub came up to hit her right temple. Then the tiled floor struck her forehead.

Her right hand made a feeble, palsied, little girl's gesture and she lost consciousness.

CHAPTER SIXTY-FIVE

ASSON changed into the priest outfit he had kept in his valise. Then he taped the valise under the row of wash basins. No one would notice it unless they deliberately stuck their head under there, looking.

As he slid the automatic into his inside breast pocket he heard the slap of two pairs of feet outside in the corridor. He climbed on top of the toilet and concentrated on breathing as quietly as possible.

He heard the door open and shut. The sound of zippers, then men making use of urinals.

"How about a brew at Foster's after we get out of here?"

"I need something. Freaks me out the way that kid jumped. I just touched him."

"Your touch probably felt like an electric shock. Get used to it."

When the door closed behind the two men it was so quiet he could hear the water passing through the pipes. The ancient building made stretching and settling sounds.

It occurred to him he wouldn't see the Berman girl till tomorrow some time. But it wouldn't matter what happened to her until after tomorrow, when he had given her aunt and uncle their lesson. Maybe he would simply kill her. Or he might keep her as a dividend, a living extension of them. He could continue to punish her for the lingering anger at them he knew he'd feel. *Wouldn't that be lov-er-ly!* he said to Her. Plenty of time to deal with the girl.

He shook the sleep from his legs.

While he waited he allowed himself to feel the need he had been resisting for the next one. He closed his eyes and saw a collage of the ones he had chosen. Saw the terror in their eyes when they realized what was to come next. Placed his cheek on cooling breasts and thighs. Tasted their tears, their blood.

He let the images flow till the pressure grew unbearable in his groin and his throat clogged with adrenaline. Then he focused his mind on the rest of the plan.

At ten-fifty he climbed off the commode. His feet stung and he rubbed them to get the circulation back. He opened the door and looked both ways.

It was quiet with a faint white light in the hallway. A woman in a white uniform was far down the corridor pushing a gurney.

Nasson tiptoed out of the bathroom closing the door quietly. Walked in the opposite direction of the woman.

He passed a women's bathroom. A locked room marked RECREATION. A series of rooms from which he heard occasional whimperings and soft sobs. A door marked CONFERENCE. Two huge doors joined together with a padlock: DINING HALL. The corridor ended.

Damn! Berman's office must be the other way, past the woman pushing the gurney.

Hearing footsteps he ran back to the bathroom on the

balls of his feet. Returned to the stall he had occupied before. Worked hard on his breathing.

The footsteps came and went.

He waited till the gurney was gone. Three fucking minutes.

There was a ringing silence in the corridor. He studied the markings on the doors as he walked by: ADMINIS-TRATION, PHARMACY, SUPPLIES, DR. JOSEPH HAAG, CLOSET, DR. KATE BERMAN.

Lov-er-ly.

But the light was on. The bitch had forgotten to shut it off. He darted to the side of the door, in case someone was inside and would see his shadow. Slowly, he turned the knob.

He took the pick gun from his pants pocket. In seconds the tumbler told him what he needed to hear.

Closed the door softly behind him. Peeled off his jacket and stuffed it along the crack at the bottom of the door.

Desk. Two chairs. File cabinets. Copy machine. Window. A green-shaded desk lamp.

He turned the light down.

Closet.

He could barely contain his excitement. He opened the closet. It was large enough to lie down and sleep in, if he curled himself up.

Are You watching? Wait, it gets better.

Excitement had filled his bladder. Suddenly his bowels insisted on being relieved. He grabbed his jacket from under the door, and left, closing the door gently behind him.

The silence rang in his ears.

The bathroom was empty—lucky. He used the same cubicle.

When he was finished he left, holding the door of the room till it closed noiselessly. As he was about to turn a voice startled him.

CHAPTER SIXTY-SIX

NASSON gripped the automatic in his pocket as he spun around.

He saw that the voice belonged to the woman who had been pushing the gurney. He had assumed her to be middle-aged. She was in her twenties.

"Didn't mean to scare you, Father. I didn't know anyone from the outside was still in the building. Not that you're an out—"

"I know what you mean. One of the patients—I'd rather not say which, you understand—"

"Sure."

"One of the patients has been having an extraordinarily hard time lately. Her mother asked me to spend extra time. I was just leaving. I wouldn't say a thing about this to anyone. Sometimes to do God's work we have to break a few rules."

She smiled, showing a glint of gold in her oatmeal face.

"Not my business. I got to go now. 'Night, Father."

"Good night, my child."

He watched her wend her way down the corridor till

she disappeared. Then he turned and walked at a normal pace to Kate Berman's office.

He decided to leave the light on low. Someone might notice if he turned it completely out. Set his watch alarm for six A.M.

He went to the closet, left the door open just enough to allow for air and lay curled on the floor.

Folding his hands on the automatic on his stomach, he closed his eyes. Allowed the collage of women to continue. Heard their voices. Best were the young ones, confronting the possibility of death for the first time.

But thoughts of Joni Freemont kept interfering.

Freak, the singer had called him.

She'll pay, he told Her.

Thoughts of the Bermans added to his growing rage.

CHAPTER SIXTY-SEVEN

WHILE Nasson slept Casey and Captain Elmendorf deployed their men.

They appeared in town one vehicle at a time
and on foot to arouse as little attention as possible.

Marksmen were on the roof of the Institute. Behind
trees in the parking lot. In view of every entrance and
exit.

When dawn came there were many more police outside the Institute than patients and staff within. Every
road leading out of town was being watched, as was the
train station.

Nasson woke before his watch sounded its alarm, not
refreshed but rested. He could taste blood. He checked
once again to see that his automatic was ready and
screwed in the silencer. It would take only seconds to kill
them, the man first because he was the biggest threat. In
moments he would be down the corridor smiling his
priest's smile and then in the parking lot of the Beekman
Arms.

He sat in the dark of the closet hearing himself breathe,
feeling the sweat extrude from his armpits.

240

Nasson savored the time, regretting its passage because he would never again have this particular anticipation.

Although he had not planned it that way, time lurched into fast-forward. Excitement built in his throat.

At eight thirty-three he heard a group of footfalls stop at the front door. A key in the lock.

They were coming to him now.

"Would you believe I left the desk light on all night," he heard Kate Berman say.

"Why wouldn't you, given the stress you're under?" a man's voice answered.

Her husband, too.

Lover-ly.

"Here, Lilah, you sit here, dear," Kate Berman said. "Josh, could you get a couple more chairs for Joni and me?"

All of them at once. Even the daughter. He tried a deep breath, settled for a shallow one.

"What's the matter, Lilah?"

He felt the singer's husky voice linger in his ears and head, crystallizing time for him. He could feel the warmth coming off her. His only regret was that his escape precluded his other need, which had been blossoming in him. There would be many others, though, with the voice.

It was so painful to wait for the medical examiner to return. *Soon they'll know my power,* he said to Her. *The newspapers, too. Everyone.*

"It's wrong. It's got to be fixed."

The excitement became unsupportable.

"What's got to be fixed?"

"Something's different," the girl said.

"Different?" the one with the voice said.

He wished the voice wasn't there to distract him from his mission.

241

"Wait a minute," Kate Berman said. "Is something wrong in this room, Lilah? The chairs? The different way the chairs are arranged? Is that bothering you, honey? Here, let's move them so they're the way they always are."

Chairs scraping on the floor grated on his ears.

"No?" Kate Berman said. "What else, dear? Too many people in my office? What's bothering you? What's different?"

"Here're your chairs," Josh Berman said returning.

"The light," the girl said. "Kate always keeps it on 150 watts. Now it's on 75."

Nasson froze. How could the girl know . . . ?

Kate Berman shouted, "He's been here!" She pressed the beeper the police had given her.

Nasson burst out of the closet.

Josh shielded all three women as he pushed them out of the room, then felt the impact of the bullet which hit him in the shoulder and spun him half way round and to the floor.

He saw a figure, all in black with a Roman collar, upon and over him. He reached up and grabbed a black-clad leg which made Nasson fall on him. Then Nasson's gun exploded in his hand. Josh felt the impact in his chest— once, twice, once again. And then there was no air or light or pain.

CHAPTER SIXTY-EIGHT

NASSON scrambled to his feet saw the motionless body and ran into the corridor, already considering possibilities, his body doing what his mind couldn't yet decide. To his left the women were nowhere to be seen. At the end of the right corridor he saw a pack of cops running toward him, automatic weapons in their hands. Swinging his head to the left he saw another pack and ran back into Kate Berman's office. Slamming the door behind him he jumped over the still body and raised the window and climbed out.

Cops. Everywhere. The staticky clack-clack of walkie-talkies.

Nasson ran faster than he'd ever run before, vaulting hedges, aware that it had started snowing and the ground was slippery.

As rifle shots reported in the air he jammed his hand into his pocket and grabbed the car keys.

Just a few more yards, he told his legs as he rounded the corner to the parking lot of the Beekman Arms. Collided with a mailman, the contact knocking precious wind from his lungs, nearly fell, caught his balance and saw the Chevy sedan.

In that millisecond when the wheels under him squealed against the slippery blacktop he knew he had been set up. They had used that bitch singer's interview on TV.

He swung the car out of the lot almost knocking down an old man in a peaked hat with a John Deere insignia.

Sirens brayed and brakes screeched as he sped through the light at the intersection of Route 9, crossing East Market Street, and sped toward Route 308 to the Taconic Parkway.

At 308 he saw two state trooper cars blocking the road, troopers positioned by them. He floored the accelerator and leaned over to the right, saw the troopers run for cover before the steering wheel pounded into his left side punching air out from his lungs leaving him dizzy. Nasson blinked the stars out of his eyes, lost focus and knocked over a mailbox. But he breathed the clarity back in, righted the car and sped on.

As he reached the Taconic he realized why he had gotten past the "roadblock" relatively easily, why so many bullets hadn't found their mark.

Looking into the rearview mirror he saw one . . . two . . . three . . . four police cars trailing him at a distance. If they were really bearing down, he would have to go a lot faster to keep ahead.

The Berman girl. They were hoping he'd lead them to her.

He smiled a distorted smile. He was safe till he got to Manhattan.

He realized why he didn't feel his usual strength. He hadn't eaten in so long that his blood sugar was low.

Reaching over to the glove compartment he grabbed

the Baggie containing the cheese and crackers and can of cola he had stashed there for an emergency.

They restored his strength.

He began constructing his strategy for when he reached Manhattan. The snow was falling heavily now. His pursuers wouldn't be able to see as well and the slippery roads would make them a little more cautious. A little leeway was all he'd need.

When his plans were made he looked into the rear view mirror, smiling. *I've got a police escort,* he said to Her.

CHAPTER SIXTY-NINE

WHEN Nasson reached the FDR Drive the snow was so heavy that traffic was very light. Still he heard no sirens, saw no attempts by the pursuing cars to move in any closer.

Suddenly it occurred to him that they might be clever enough to block off all the exits, trapping him on the Drive.

No, they still needed to know where the Berman girl was. And they assumed correctly that even if they were brilliant enough to catch him, he would never be persuaded to tell.

He had read in the *Times* the other day that the FBI was researching an additional procedure on DNA profiling. Even with insufficient amounts of DNA on the victim they would be able to get a positive identification from a wad of gum, a sweat stain or even a few cells deposited in saliva on the back of a postage stamp. He didn't chew gum or smoke and he certainly wouldn't ever be careless enough to send a traceable note to the police or newspapers.

But he did perspire. After he eluded these fools he

would immediately go to work designing an outfit that would contain his perspiration while letting him enjoy the ones he chose.

Just before the Houston Street exit he took out the automatic and laid it on his lap.

After coming off the ramp he felt even more confident. He had had to learn about Rhinebeck from maps and asking questions. Now he was in a city he knew well.

He reviewed his plan.

When he reached Fifth Avenue he made a left turn.

Fifth and Fourteenth Street.

Only two and a half blocks more.

Thirteenth.

Twelfth.

Now.

He activated his electric window, brought up the automatic, stuck his head out, turned, aimed and pressed the trigger. The bullet made a neat hole through the windshield of the car behind him and hit the woman driver. She slumped forward on her horn, her car careening off to the left. Cars behind her jammed on their brakes. Slipped and slid.

Nasson slowed his car down, reached over and opened the door on the passenger side then tumbled out of the moving vehicle.

Getting to his feet he crouched, wiping the snow from his eyes. Shot a black taxi driver who had slowed down.

The taxi came up the sidewalk, knocking down a fire hydrant which immediately began to geyser. His own car hit a pedestrian. The police cars were at least half a block away.

He sprinted to Eleventh Street, turned right, and down a few houses to number 24.

He turned the key and was inside. Locked the door.

Masterful, wasn't it?

CHAPTER SEVENTY

CASEY hung up his car phone. He turned to Kate. "Josh—I didn't want to say anything till I knew he was all right."

"What! When I didn't see him, I thought he was with the troopers."

"No, Nasson shot him in the shoulder and the chest a few times. Even with the bullet proof vest the impact knocked the wind out of him. That's all, though."

"Truth, Case?"

"God is my witness."

The phone rang.

"Chief?"

"Yeah. Where is he?"

"A man in our lead car popped his head out just in time. Nasson ran onto Eleventh Street."

"Good man! I'm three blocks away. I want Eleventh Street covered down to the river. Start knocking on doors from Fifth down and from the water on up. No one answers the bell, get in anyhow!"

"Anyhow?"

"Is there an impediment in my speech? Break glass,

shoot the fucking lock off. I'm responsible. We're fighting the clock. I want a net around the whole Village. Any cop brings him in is going to be the next Audie Murphy. Any fuck-up is going to be on the leather bar shift the rest of his life."

"The Commissioner's on the phone."

"I can't be reached. *Go.* Over."

Kate said, "C'mon, let's go get Jenny."

Nasson drained his glass of Scotch. Yes, he would design a new outfit so that even when they perfected the new DNA profiling he couldn't be identified. But the technology was catching up. No more ego. Let them think the copycats were him. From now on he would concentrate on only what mattered. He would fly to Boston, Washington, Los Angeles. Buy a knife at Walmarts, find the next one and enjoy her, fly home the same night. A different city every time. Then there was Europe and beyond. They would never suspect, let alone catch him.

Now what do You think of me?

But they would never find him here, either. Not if he stayed in the secret room with her. After a few days they would assume he had escaped the area.

Then he would really escape. Maybe even take the Bermans' bitch with him. Send them cards from Europe and the Orient. Stew themselves to death.

He opened the door to the secret room and was alarmed till he found her on the bathroom floor. He hoped she hadn't ruined his plan now by dying.

Casey, Kate at his side, stood in the middle of a huddle of police at the corner of Fifth and Eleventh.

"Sergeant," he said, "you and your men check the odd

numbers across the street. I'll take the even with my men. Hurry!"

Nasson checked her heart. Alive. He carried her to the bed and brought her some water. It dribbled down her face. All the color was gone from her skin and her hair hung down like a mop.

He threw the rest of the contents of the cup in her face.

An eye twitched. Then another.

Jenny opened her eyes. It was as if she had been reduced to an intuition. She lay awaiting her body's return. A current of heat came and went, threatening unconsciousness. From somewhere came a vaguely familiar voice.

"Did you miss me? Hope dinner's ready. Murderous day. You look absolutely parched."

The words made no sense to her. Where had the exhaustion and the scalding heat come from? If she didn't drink water soon she'd die.

While he was in the bathroom refilling the cup, what he heard next made him stop, put down the cup, shut the faucet.

He heard it once more. Could his ears be playing tricks on him?

"Water please . . ."

The *voice*. The Bermans' niece had developed the *voice*. It couldn't be true. Lucky as he was, he hadn't dreamed of this.

He delighted in the heightened sensation that emerged as a result of the adrenaline and ice that now tingled in his arteries—the smoothness of the cup imprinted on his fingers, the quivering along the inside of his thighs, the awareness of the roots of his teeth, the coiled muscles in his back, the tug at his groin.

* * *

Casey's walkie-talkie crackled.

"What?" he said.

"Nothing so far, Chief."

"Where are you?"

"We just got out of the brownstone after the church at the corner."

"Hurry, dammit, I'm up to number 18 already."

"C'mon, Case," Kate said.

The excitement was a weight between Nasson's legs.

At the entrance to her room, with a gaze as sharp and clean as polished brass, he saw her look at him and see in his eyes what awaited her. There was nothing better than their look when they first knew. As good, but nothing better.

There was no room in his head now for anything but a Berman with the voice. When she tried to rise he came through the open doorway and was on her.

He hit her across the head and she grabbed his hand and bit. Where did she get such a reserve of strength? He punched her straight in her face. She slumped over. Stopped moving. A trickle of blood ran out the corner of her mouth. He lapped at it with his tongue.

He rose, ran his hand over the top of his head feeling the growth. He would shave his head and check carefully for any growth on his body. He went to the bathroom and turned on a faucet in the sink.

"Chief!"

"I'm listening."

"We got him!"

"Where are you?"

"Number 19. We heard a young girl scream. Brownstone. Hard rock on so loud he can't hear us banging on the outside door.

"Go in. Now! We'll be backing you up."

Jenny's eyes opened. The pain in her face stunned her. When she remembered where she was she tried to raise herself up. Her weakness made it feel as though the laws of gravity had changed.

Finally, she crawled off the bed. Dragged herself along the floor. She could hear water running from the bathroom. If she could only make it to a window in the living room she could throw something at the glass so somebody down in the street might hear . . .

Kate and Casey stood gawking in the doorway of the first floor apartment in number 19. Surrounded by uniforms was a naked girl in her early twenties. Her hands were cuffed behind her back. There were red welts on her buttocks and the backs of her legs. Next to her was a sinewy man wearing a matching black leather hood and a matching pouch between his legs.

"Christ help us!" Casey said, then ran out of the building after Kate.

Nasson toweled away the last of the shaving cream. He opened the medicine cabinet, removed the box of cotton gauze and pressed down on the aluminum button underneath. The chest swung open revealing the compartment he had built behind it.

He reached in and took out the splint. Fitted it into his mouth. Jammed on the surgical gloves. He broke open a small blister package and slipped on a condom.

When he turned a noise came from the living room.

I love their futile struggles, don't You?

He stalked out.

Jenny had just managed to raise the ginger jar lamp over her head with both hands to smash it through the window when she suddenly felt her head being pulled back by her hair.

Dropping the lamp, she felt his knuckles bash her lips against her teeth. She fell backward. A moment passed. Her head began to clear. When she could see him clearly again he had his knuckles pressed to his mouth, sucking her blood from them. His smile was a grotesque contortion of his mouth, her blood staining his plastic teeth.

She opened her mouth to scream but her voice was muffled by a hand that smelled ludicrously of limes. Then a metallic-like finger was pressing at the back of her neck. She felt herself growing smaller and smaller. Finally, she disappeared.

Kate peered through a glass panel of the entrance door to the brownstone that was number 24.

"No names on any of the mailboxes," she whispered to Casey and the police beside them. "Four boxes and no names."

"And there're lights on the top floor," Casey said quietly.

"Right," Kate whispered. "This could be it."

Breathing heavily Nasson tore her shirt open, sending buttons over the bed. All his senses were exquisitely keen.

Her parted lips made him feel she was drawing a finger

253

just below his navel. Her violet lids were closed, as if she were glutted with desire. He soaked up the smell of her, felt the warmth emitting from her, felt a tightening in his testicles.

"I can smell your cunt, do you know that?"

He snapped the bra over her head. Unsnapped and unzipped her jeans. Dragged her jeans down off her legs and threw them aside.

She had the breasts of a girl but even through her panties he could see a woman's full bush. He tore the crotch of the panties with his teeth, then ripped the rest out with his hands.

Reached and rubbed her pubic hair.

"Don't open your eyes," he said deliciously, "Carl's got a surprise for you."

He rose, threw the door open and marched to the kitchen. Opened a drawer. Stood deciding which knife.

Casey took out a handkerchief, wrapped it round the butt of his revolver and broke the glass. Reached in and unbolted the door.

"Koenig, cover this door, case he's here and gets past us. Valassis, you go on up ahead and take the roof. Kate, you'd better—"

"I'm going with you," she said taking her gun from her purse.

Nasson had just chosen a cleaver when he heard a sound.

Above. Someone on the roof. *Police.*

He blinked his eyes tight, straining to hear better.

Footsteps coming up the stairs.

Considered running to the secret room. Too late. No

time to get his automatic, either. He jammed himself in behind the kitchen door. Sucked in his breath.

A moment, two at most, then footsteps inside the apartment. A blessing he couldn't retrieve his automatic. Shots would alert the cops on the roof.

He raised the cleaver over his head. Waited.

Casey made furious motions with his hands to tell Kate to stay behind him. But she knew it made no sense to allow themselves to become one target.

Casey made his way along the hallway that led to the kitchen. Kate took the one leading to the bedrooms.

Nasson saw the barrel of a gun sticking out, like a robot monster's finger. Slammed the cleaver onto the weapon and knocked it to the floor. Kicked it away.

Kate's entire body lunged forward with the noise. She ran.

Nasson saw that it was Casey. Threw a chop to his head. The detective was already bending for his gun, so Nasson's hand struck only his shoulder. Casey thudded to the floor. Nasson raised the cleaver.

Kate rounded the corner. Saw Nasson holding the cleaver high above Casey.

No time.

She extended her gun. Moved forward. Fast.

255

She hesitated. She knew little about guns. What if she missed and hit Casey?

She looked up at the cleaver. Then dredged up the words huskily.

"It's Aunt Amanda, Carl."

Nasson heard Her voice. Turned.

Kate squeezed the trigger, was thrown backward by the explosion.

Missed.

She saw as if in a series of penny-arcade pictures all run together Casey scramble for his gun Nasson run at her with blood erupting from his nose and mouth as Casey's bullet hit its mark. Saw Nasson's legs kick out from under him as Casey's next round broke his back.

Nasson was crawling toward her, his right hand moving over his face as if trying to restore his features. The hydraulic pressure of Casey's bullet on his brain fluid had made Nasson's head swell to the size of a lion's. Part of her breakfast sprang up her throat.

Finally he lay stilled.

She ran to find Jenny.

EPILOGUE

AFTER an early Sunday dinner Casey left the Bermans' home to pick up his daughter, his son-in-law and his new grandson at Kennedy.

Josh went to his observatory.

He scanned the April sky, grateful to the Pleiades for having delivered again on their promise of a shift in fortune. Jenny was safe and back in school. Kate was teaching a course about violent crime at John Jay College of Criminal Justice. More important, she was over her fears enough to have returned to being a consultant to police departments about serial killers.

After a time he heard something and turned away from the telescope. Kate and Jenny were standing there arm in arm, smiling through the wear the winter's crises had lent to their faces.

A brief, faraway look passed over Jenny's eyes, a sadness. His throat constricted. She was suffering and would suffer more. But she was mending in therapy. And he and Kate had more than enough love to help heal the damage.

"Do you think," Jenny said, "there's life up there somewhere?"

"Somewhere. Only ego makes us think we're the only ones in the universe."

He went over and stood close to them.

"I'll tell you, though. Whatever kind of life it is can take lessons from you two. Not all the stars are in the sky."